What NOT to Do When You Find a Spaceship

Drake Highlander

AuthorHouse™
1663 Liberty Drive, Suite 200
Bloomington, IN 47403
www.authorhouse.com
Phone: 1-800-839-8640

© *2009 Drake Highlander. All rights reserved.*

No part of this book may be reproduced, stored in a retrieval system, or transmitted by any means without the written permission of the author.

First published by AuthorHouse 3/27/2009

ISBN: 978-1-4389-0744-4

Library of Congress Control Number: 2008907294

Printed in the United States of America
Bloomington, Indiana

This book is printed on acid-free paper.

For Seressia, whose coaching and encouragement

have made all the difference.

Contents

Don't Go Into the Woods at Night	1
Don't Tell Your Friends	21
Whatever You Do, Don't Touch It	45
Don't Try to Fly It, Stupid	55
Don't Get Eaten	63
Avoid Getting Pulverized	87
Don't Feed the Monsters	97
Don't Trust the Aliens	111
Try Not to Die If You Can Help It	127
Don't Look Into the Light	157
Epilogue	173

Don't Go Into the Woods at Night

Tommy Steiber woke to the sound of distant thunder, and he knew right away that he was in trouble. He'd fallen asleep over his work again. He jumped up from his chair and closed the window. As he did, wind gusted through the opening, scattering papers and art supplies across his desk. An old glass of water tipped over, drowning his work.

"Ah, great! That's just great," he complained as he mopped up the water with his sweatshirt. Colors, mostly red and gold, smeared across the pages.

Thunder rumbled again.

Tommy left the mess and ran to the back door. Just like he thought, he'd left the doggie door unlocked, and Cujo was nowhere in sight.

"I'm headed back to work," said Mom, grabbing her purse off the kitchen counter.

Tommy's jaw dropped open. "The night shift, again?"

She smiled apologetically, and ruffled his hair. "Trash and laundry, Blue Eyes. I need a clean uniform for tomorrow, and you need clean boxers."

Tommy caught sight of the overflowing garbage can in the kitchen and the mountain of dirty laundry on the washer, and he groaned. "Mom, why can't we get a dryer like everyone else? We're not in the 1950s. It's 1975!"

"First, let me get the car fixed. Then we'll talk about a dryer. Tips have been horrible lately. It's like that every summer." Mom pushed the kitchen window curtain aside and peered at the darkening sky. "We're supposed to get a break from the rain tomorrow, so get the wet clothes hung out early in the morning, okay? I'll be home by nine."

Lightning flashed outside. Tommy bit his lip, hoping she wouldn't ask.

"Where's Cujo?"

"Asleep in my room," he lied.

Mom's eyes saddened as she wrapped her arm around him. "He's been sleeping a lot more lately, hasn't he?"

Tommy looked away, trying not to think about it. "He's fine Mom."

"That old mutt's been good to you, Tommy, but he won't live forever," she said, hugging him.

He hugged her back, letting the tears come.

After several long moments, she sighed, and brushed his hair from his forehead. "Better lock the doggie door just in case he gets up. You know how he likes to go out when it rains. I swear if he drags any more mud in here, we could grow crops."

Beep! Beep! blared a car horn from the street.

"That's my ride." She planted a kiss on his forehead before leaving. "I'll bring home some breakfast for you in the morning. No writing till your chores are done."

Tommy nodded, wiping his eyes.

The second the front door closed, he snatched Cujo's leash and a flashlight. Then he dashed out the back door. He nearly collided with little Danny Muglyn, who was climbing the back porch steps. "Not now, Danny," he grouched. "Cujo! Here boy!"

"I just have one question," said Danny in a squeaky voice that matched his size and age. "Then I'll stop being a pest."

"You'll never stop being a pest. Go home. It's almost dark, and another storm's coming." Tommy jogged down the steps, scanning the back yard. "Have you seen Cujo?"

Danny chuckled. "Nope, I haven't seen the *ugliest dog in the world*. That's what Mitch calls him."

"Yeah, well, Mitch is a big jerk." Tommy grabbed Danny's arm. "Do *not* tell him I said that."

"I promise, but you gotta let me have a peek at the next issue."

"I told you yesterday that it's not ready. Besides, I just spilled water all over it."

"Why did you do that?"

"Because I like ruining my comic books, that's why! Now go home!" demanded Tommy, shoving Danny away from the house. The little boy walked away with his head hung low as gusts of wind brought the smell of rain.

Tommy sighed. "Come on, Dan Man. I'll walk you home, and you can ask me your question."

"Cool!" said Danny, bouncing up and down. "What I want to know is why—"

"Thomas Steiber, I have a bone to pick with you," came a salty voice from over the backyard fence. "My metal detector is missing again. I'd expect a twelve-year-old to be more responsible."

Tommy couldn't help rolling his eyes. "I didn't take it, Mr. Beaker. I've *never* taken it."

Old Man Beaker's head seemed to hover just above the wooden slats of the fence. "Well then, explain to me how, every time, it just reappears in *your* yard, all covered in mud. Hmmm? You can tell your mother that I want it replaced this time."

Tommy scoffed in protest. "Replaced? But Mr. Beaker..."

The floating head was gone.

"One day, I'm gonna live in a log cabin away from everyone and just write comic books," vowed Tommy as he and Danny left the backyard.

"Can I help?" asked Danny. "I'm a really fast learner."

"No. Now what's your question?"

"Well, what I don't get is why the Space Elves tried to stop the Doom Droids at the end of issue twelve? That's crazy. The Droids saved the Elves from certain destruction by the Galactic Goblins."

"You gotta *read* the comic, Dan. You can't just look at the pictures."

"I did. Lord Xorweld said the Droids were out of control, but I think they were just doing their job."

Tommy shook his head. "The Droids weren't following orders anymore. The Elves had no choice; they had to shut 'em down."

"What do you mean, they had no choice? You write the stories. You can give them a choice."

"That's not how it works," said Tommy, his stomach twisting with guilt. No matter how many times he tried to rewrite the story, it always came out the same: The Doom Droids would rise up against their creators and bring an end to the Space Elves. Nothing in the galaxy could save the noble people. The only idea he had—The Elf of Light—wasn't working. It was too far out there. His readers would never believe it.

A lone drop of rain struck Tommy's face as the two boys approached the Muglyn's house. Mrs. Muglyn was just pulling into the driveway in her old station wagon. She and one of her daughters quickly got out and began unloading groceries. Tommy started when he realized the girl was Muggie. She didn't seem to notice him.

Mrs. Muglyn admonished Danny for being outside with a storm approaching and loaded him down with paper grocery bags. "Good to see you, Thomas," she said, handing Tommy some groceries. "How's your Mom? Take those inside, would you, dear?"

"I got 'em," said Muggie, as she took the bags from Tommy. She didn't even look at him.

"Bye Tommy," called Danny as he went inside. "Thanks for walking me home. I'll come over tomorrow."

As the Muglyns went inside, Tommy headed for the woods.

"Where are you going?" asked Muggie from the front porch.

Tommy turned, walking backwards. "I gotta find Cujo."

Muggie walked back down the porch steps, grocery bags in hand. "Tommy, that dog can take care of himself. Come inside before it starts to rain."

"Too late," said Tommy, as drops began popping all around them.

"Are you crazy? You'll get struck by lightning."

Tommy smiled inside. It was like the good old days. There she stood, rain pelting her fiery red curls, acting like his older sister.

"Carrie Anne, come inside," called Mrs. Muglyn.

Tommy walked away. "See ya, Muggie."

"Go home, Steiber," he heard her yell.

* * *

Tommy cut though several yards as he jogged to the edge of the woods. Luckily, the storm looming overhead seemed to be grazing his neighborhood; most of the rain and lightning were farther south. The last thing he needed, going into Deep Creek Woods, was heavy rain.

What NOT to Do When You Find a Spaceship

The rolling slope that made up the northern side of the woods gave way to Lothlem Gorge about a half mile in. The area near the edge of the gorge was prone to mud slides, especially in times of heavy rainfall. That's exactly where Cujo would be; Tommy was certain.

Cujo liked to dig holes near the gorge. Tommy figured he'd discovered an old Cherokee burial ground or something, though he never came home with any bones. Tommy didn't believe the neighborhood theory that the old dog was disturbed, or that he had "doggie Alzheimer's." Cujo was smarter than most people. He had the most intelligent eyes. Sometimes, he even seemed to know what Tommy was thinking.

Lighting struck much closer, making Tommy worry that the storm had changed course. He stopped; getting struck by lightning wasn't on his list of things to do. Glancing back up the slope, the neighborhood streetlights looked like tiny stars twinkling through the wall of trees.

Tommy resumed his trek, going as fast as he dared down the slope. The dim light from the flashlight was just enough to navigate the rocks and fallen trees.

Why his old mutt insisted on going out during stormy weather, Tommy had no idea. Any other day, Muggie would've been right—Cujo was the toughest of dogs and could take care of himself. But lately, he'd been moving slowly and sleeping almost all the time.

"Cujooo!" called Tommy, tears gathering in his eyes. He wasn't going to let his dog die out here, alone in the woods. He owed him more than that—so much more.

With a shudder, Tommy recalled the day he'd met Cujo two years ago. Mitch Steelmaker had cornered Tommy in the woods and was about to give him the beating he'd long promised. Out of nowhere this mud-covered creature appeared by his side, teeth bared at Mitch, growling viciously. When Tommy realized that it was defending him, he didn't care what sort of beast it was. He'd walked away from the confrontation without a scratch, and Cujo had followed him home. They'd been best friends ever since.

Tommy slowed down. He was getting close to the gorge. Here, the land dipped into several steep ravines before dropping away for good, like giant stairs leading down to the edge of a cliff. This is where the mud slides occurred; the worst ones carried the land, trees and all, down into the gorge.

"Cujo? Cuuujooo!"

Tommy listened for Cujo's signature howl. Cujo never barked; he howled. As ugly as he was, he could howl like a virtuoso.

Stepping down into a ravine, Tommy saw holes, but they were old ones. He came over a small rise and climbed down into another ravine, then up and down into another. There was no sign of Cujo.

What if he was wrong? What if his old dog had gone back home? Tommy shivered beneath his wet clothes. His shoes were clumps of red clay, and the flashlight batteries were failing.

He called one last time, "Cuuuuujooooo!" Only the wind and rain responded, as the storm grew stronger.

Tommy turned to leave.

A thick flash of lightning lit the woods for a long moment. Something shiny caught his eye. He jogged to the far edge of the ravine and picked up Mr. Beaker's metal detector. His face wrinkled in puzzlement. There was something else on the ground. He reached down, touched a shovel. Looking around, he saw fresh holes.

"Cujo!" called Tommy, his heart pumping hard in his chest. If someone else was out here...

A soft howl cut through the wind and rain; a series of tones that could only be his dog's.

"Where are ya, boy?"

Tommy followed the song to the edge of a shallow hole. Cujo was there on the ground, his form barely visible in the darkness. But something was wrong; he didn't look right, and he wasn't moving.

Warm tears mixed with the rain falling on Tommy's face. "I'm sorry, boy. This is all my fault." He reached down to pick up his dog.

Flash! Flash! Flash! Lightning struck like a strobe light. In that instant, Tommy saw a grotesque figure where his dog should have been. He stumbled backward and fell.

Thunder echoed through the woods.

Tommy lay glued to the soggy ground, his blood thrumming through his veins. The creature continued to howl, sounding just like Cujo. Slowly, Tommy convinced himself that he hadn't actually seen what he thought he saw: a man-like monster covered in mud. He gave his flashlight a whack, and fresh light poured from the lens.

Shocked anew, Tommy stared in horror at the beast before him. The eyes that bore into him were Cujo's, but the rest of it...

The creature reached out for Tommy with a clawed hand. Tommy stared at that hand, and his heart beat even faster. Cujo's paws had always looked odd, even claw-like. His face had always been strange, even for a dog—like a bulldog with oversized eyes, almost like...an alien?

Tommy scrambled to his feet and took several steps back. All of the long hours writing comic book stories about Space Elves and their enemies were finally getting to him. He had to be hallucinating, or was he?

"C-Cujo? Is that you, boy?"

The creature strained its muddy arm to reach Tommy, howling mournful notes through ragged breaths.

Looking closer at the creature's face, Tommy realized it looked a lot like Cujo, but without a snout. Even its skin was Cujo's tawny color. This *thing* was his dog, but how could that be? Tommy looked around, remembering the metal detector and shovel. Understanding washed through him. But as one mystery was solved, another took its place: What was Cujo looking for?

Tommy stepped closer, his eyes straining as the flashlight's glow weakened. He reached for the creature's outstretched hand, but stopped short.

"I don't understand. What happened to you?"

Cujo gasped for air, and then exhaled long and slow, like a balloon deflating. His outstretched arm dropped to the ground. His eyelids closed over pupils fixed on Tommy.

"No!" cried Tommy, grabbing Cujo's limp hand. "Don't die like this, Cujo! Please don't go. You have to tell me what this is all about. What does this mean? *Who are you?*"

The sound of rain and distant thunder filled the woods. Cujo didn't respond.

A glow, barely visible, appeared around the dog-creature's body. It grew stronger as it spread to Tommy, wrapping around him like his mother's warm embrace. The dark woods fell away as he lost himself in the light. Fuzzy shapes appeared in the brightness. They seemed light years away, but racing closer. Then, with a rush of pain and color, the shapes slammed into Tommy's mind—planets, spaceships, battles...*Elves!*

Pressure rose behind his eyes, like a colossal ice cream headache. The woods swayed back and forth. Tommy fought to stay awake. He needed to see more. As consciousness pulled away from him in a swirl of light and darkness, he saw a golden angel.

Don't Tell Your Friends

Shapechanger was Tommy's first thought when he woke. Aspirin was his second. The serenity of the morning woods, with its chirping birds and scampering squirrels, did nothing to ease his aching head.

Tommy slowly rolled himself over, coming face-to-face with Cujo's corpse. He suddenly discovered that it was possible to be really sad and really freaked out at the same time. Cujo had been his dog by day and this hole-digging alien by night. What else could he be other than a shapechanger—a creature that could alter its form to look like other beings?

When Tommy stood up, his forehead throbbed with pain. With his head in his hands, he recalled the images he'd seen in the light from Cujo's body. Stories were playing in fast forward—*his* stories from his comic books. But he saw them as they were actually happening; as if they were real life events and not cartoon drawings.

Straining his memory, like recalling a fading dream, Tommy tried to remember his last thought before passing out. It was something important, though he didn't know why. Reaching through the pain in his head to the back of his mind, Tommy groped for the thought he knew was there. He could almost see it.

Voices broke the tranquility of the woods and Tommy's concentration all at once. He spun around, listening like a frightened animal. He heard kids' voices, probably Mitch and his gang, but with all the hills and ravines, it was difficult to tell how close they were.

Tommy grabbed the shovel, jumped down into the hole next to Cujo's body, and started digging. He wasn't going to let Mitch or anyone else find Cujo and dissect his body. The shovel struck something hard almost immediately. He tried a few more times with no better luck. "Solid rock. That's just great!"

Stepping out of the hole and moving father up the slope, Tommy struggled to dig a shallow grave under a tall pine. The clay was soft but heavy, making his muscles burn with the effort.

The voices grew louder.

There was no time for ceremony. Tommy dragged Cujo's body into the hole and covered it with mud and debris from the forest floor. Hoping that the grave was sufficiently camouflaged, he headed home with the metal detector and shovel in hand. He'd just climbed out of the last ravine and was on his way up the slope when someone called his name.

"Yo, Tommy!" shouted Chuckey from atop an adjacent hill. Chuckey Peats had been his first best friend. He was also an idiot. No doubt he was there with Mitch Steelmaker. Tommy groaned. Couldn't Chuckey just keep his mouth shut for once?

Tommy broke into a jog in an effort to get out of the woods before Mitch caught him.

"Where ya goin'?" called Chuckey

"Yeah, Tommy, where ya goin'?" asked Scott Salinas as he stepped out from behind a tree, blocking Tommy's way.

Scott had grown even taller since Tommy had seen him last. Otherwise, he looked the same: short black hair, giant backpack full of who-knew-what, and eyes that gave no clue as to what he'd do next.

"Eagle One to scouts," came Mitch's voice from a walkie-talkie in Scott's hand. "Report in."

Scott raised the walkie-talkie to his mouth and hesitated before saying, "Nothing to report, Captain."

"Thanks," said Tommy, as a cool sweat came over him.

Scott stuffed the radio into his backpack. "Mitch is over by the creek, so you're safe for now."

"I saw a dead raccoon," Chuckey said into his walkie-talkie as he approached. He was out of breath from his short run and more out of shape than ever. Blond hair sprouted from his head in all directions, and his big cheeks smiled. "Hey Tommy, what happened to you?"

"You look like you got in a fight with a mud wrestler," said Scott.

"Yeah, something like that," said Tommy, unable to hold back a grin. It was like old times, when the three of them explored the woods with Muggie. He continued his hike up the slope as Chuckey and Scott followed.

"Tommy, when are you gonna be done with issue thirteen of Loremasters?" begged Chuckey.

Tommy's mind filled with images of embattled Space Elves. "I wish I knew."

"Scott says the stories are too unrealistic."

"That's because he's a brainiac," said Tommy. "He needs a scientific explanation for everything."

Scott shrugged. "I mean, really, Tommy, the Doom Droids wouldn't waste time *capturing* the Elves, they'd just blast 'em to—"

"The Droids are programmed to *protect* the Elves," explained Tommy.

"So they imprison them in crystallox instead?" The tall boy scoffed. "That's lame."

Tommy tried to change the subject. "What are you guys doing out here?"

"We're looking for a place to build a fort," said Chuckey.

Scott gave the plump boy a sour look. "And Mitch told you to keep it secret."

"Private Peats!" hollered Mitch over Chuckey's walkie-talkie, startling him. "Where are you, soldier?"

"I'm over here with Scott and Tommy," Chuckey answered into his radio.

Tommy exhaled sharply. "Great! Just fantastic. Thanks Chuck! Now he knows I'm here."

Chuckey looked bewildered. "What did I do?"

"Tommy, you'd better go east if you wanna avoid a close encounter of the painful kind," said Scott.

"Too late," said Tommy when Mitch appeared over a rise further up the slope. The older boy strutted toward the group, wearing his usual camouflage pants, black T-shirt, and bulging biceps. Nausea settled into Tommy's stomach. There was no escape this time.

Mitch pointed to Chuckey. "Peats, drop and give me ten. Your orders were to go a hundred yards *west*, and then report."

"Yes sir," said Chuckey, groaning through each push-up.

"Map," said Mitch to no one in particular. Scott pulled a hand-drawn map out of his backpack and handed it to him. Mitch studied the map. "How ya been, Steiber?"

Tommy's brain switched to *pause* for several seconds. Mitch was being nice? "Good," he blurted. "I've been good."

"What are you doing in the woods?" asked Mitch, still not looking at him.

Tommy racked his brain for an explanation. "Just exploring. You know, getting back to nature. Definitely *not* building a fort, if that's what you're thinking."

"Peats! Make it twenty," ordered Mitch. Chuckey moaned in response. Mitch folded the map and stepped into Tommy's personal space. "Don't lie to me, Steiber." He brushed some dried mud off Tommy's shoulder. "You've obviously been busy doing something in my woods. Tell me what it is."

Tommy nodded his head slightly. *This* was the Mitch he knew and hated. It didn't matter what Tommy said. Mitch would find a way to turn it into an argument and a fight. He was going to get beaten up, and Scott and Chuckey couldn't help him.

"My dog died," said Tommy, gambling. "So I buried him in the woods, that's all."

"Aw, Cujo died?" asked Chuckey between push-ups. "That's too bad."

"Yeah," said Mitch sympathetically.

For a second Tommy thought his gamble had paid off. An instant later Mitch had him by his shirt collar. "Too bad that hellhound's not around to save you. He nearly bit my leg off last time."

"Get off me!" demanded Tommy.

Scott moved beside them. "Take it easy, Mitch."

"Stay out of this, Lieutenant," ordered Mitch. "If there's one thing I can't stand, Steiber, it's a liar. Why would you need a metal detector to bury a dog? You found something in *my* woods and dug it up."

"Oh, like buried treasure!" said Chuckey, scrambling to his feet.

Mitch's eyes lit up with greed. "Where is it?" he demanded, threatening Tommy with a clenched fist.

Tommy's vision filled with stars, and the ground beneath him swayed. He forced himself to breath. "All right, I'll tell you where it is."

"No. You'll *show* us where it is," said Mitch with a smirk. "You'll lead us to it."

There was only one thing Tommy could show them that might satisfy Mitch's curiosity, but there was no way he was going to reveal Cujo's burial place. So he played the only card he had—his ace in the hole—but he could only use it once.

"Is that a snake?" asked Tommy, looking at the ground next to Mitch.

"Where?" Mitch screeched, jumping around like an Irish dancer on fire. Mitch hated snakes, and everyone knew it.

Tommy dropped the tools and ran for his life. He was halfway up the slope when he heard Mitch yell, "I'll get you, Steiber. If you ever step foot in my woods again, I'll bloody ya good!"

* * *

Walking through his neighborhood, Tommy wondered if he'd ever see Deep Creek Woods again; not as long as Mitch was around.

The eighth grade flunkout always found a way to ruin everything. Scott used to say that Mitch boasted about joining the Army when he turned sixteen. Tommy's heart soared at the thought of life without Mitch in the neighborhood.

His reverie evaporated. From down the street, he spied Old Man Beaker at the front door of his house talking to Mom. His internal *I'm in big trouble* meter kicked in. How could he explain that an alien had taken the geezer's metal detector? Mr. Beaker walked away from the house, looking pleased with himself. That wasn't a good sign.

Thankful that he'd remembered to kick off his shoes before running inside, Tommy found his mom in the kitchen washing dishes. His meter cranked up a notch when he noticed the empty garbage can, and again upon hearing the clothes washer running.

"Mom, I'm *very* sorry." She continued her kitchen cleaning as if he wasn't there. Her stern expression made her look so much older. "Mom, I know this is what you do when you're really, really mad at me, but if you'll let me explain—"

"I have just enough time to catch a few hours' sleep before going back to work," she said coolly, handing him a basket of wet laundry. "While you're hanging that out, think about how you're going to pay for Mr. Beaker's metal detector."

"But I didn't take it," protested Tommy as she walked away. "Mom!"

"Your breakfast is in the fridge," she said before closing the door to her room.

* * *

Tommy attacked the laundry, pinning the garments on the clothesline with ferocity, still reeling from everything that had happened.

Cujo was an alien who'd tried to tell him something before he died. The Space Elves he'd been writing about were possibly real, and here he was dodging bullies and hanging laundry. Okay, there was only one bully.

"Hey," said a sweet voice. Tommy turned to find Muggie walking up to him. She was practically dressed up, with her designer jeans and matching blouse. Gone were the dingy shorts and worn out sneakers she used to wear.

"Why are you looking at me like that?" she asked, her hazel eyes skeptical.

"You look nice, that's all."

"Whatever. Have you seen Danny?"

"Not since last night."

Muggie frowned. "What happened to you? Did you find Cujo?"

"I found him." Tommy stabbed another clothespin on the line. "He died, so I buried him out in the woods."

"I'm sorry, Tommy." She actually sounded like it. "I know Cujo was old and everything, but still..."

"He's all right," said Tommy, as tears threatened his eyes. Danny showed up just in time.

"Mitch is a big jerk!" the second-grader complained as he plopped down in the grass.

"There you are," said Muggie, ruffling his nut-colored hair. "Danny, you know you can't hang around the older boys."

"I just wanted to see what they found, that's all."

Tommy dropped the basket of laundry and sat down next to Danny. "*Please* tell me they found a place to build a fort."

Danny shook his head. "No, they were digging something up."

"Oh, great!" cried Tommy, slamming his fists on the ground. "That's just awesome! They must have found Cujo's body. They better not be digging him up."

Muggie made a face. "That's sick. Why would they dig up your old dog?"

"No, it's something metal and shiny," insisted Danny, "something big!"

"Something metal?" Tommy jumped to his feet. "I don't believe this. They must have found what Cujo was searching for."

"Tommy, what's going on?" asked Muggie.

"You know how Cujo was always digging near the gorge?" he explained, walking toward the woods.

"No," said Muggie, following him. "I haven't been in the woods since I was eleven."

"Well, I think he was looking for something..." Tommy wasn't sure how much he should tell her. "Let me ask you a question. Do you believe in extraterrestrial life?"

Muggie laughed openly. "You expect me to believe that Cujo dug up an alien? Tommy, I don't read comic books."

"You guys go ahead without me," called Danny from his spot in the grass. "Mitch said he'd break my thumbs if I came back, and I need these bad boys for video games."

Tommy stopped cold. "I can't go back there. Mitch promised to rearrange my face just this morning."

"C'mon, Tommy, I can handle Mitch Steelmaker," Muggie told him as she marched toward the woods.

Tommy couldn't believe it. Muggie knew firsthand how violent Mitch could be. Yet, there she was, headed for another confrontation with the brute. Fortunately, by the time they'd trekked down the slope to the lower ravines, Tommy had convinced Muggie to try to be sneaky.

Hiding behind a tree, Tommy took a cautious look around. His heart sank as he realized that Mitch had the others digging in the same hole Cujo had started the night before. It looked like they'd found a smooth silver sphere the size of a small car.

"What *is* that?" Muggie whispered.

"I don't know," Tommy whispered back, his heart pounding. "Whatever it is, I think it's what Cujo was trying to dig up."

"I want a closer look," said Muggie, stepping out of their hiding place and down into the ravine before Tommy could stop her. "Hey, Rambo! What's in the ditch?"

Mitch stared at her for several seconds, his mouth hanging open.

"Hey there, Muggie," said Chuckey.

Scott leaned on his shovel. "I told you Danny would rat on us."

"Muggie?" Mitch said finally. "Aren't you a little overdressed for the woods? Why don't you run along and get your nails done or whatever you do. Me and my men have work to do."

"Not to question your *military intelligence*," said Muggie, "but you know, that could be a bomb."

Chuckey dropped his shovel and clambered out of the hole.

"Keep digging, Private," ordered Mitch. "We'll take a break when we reach halfway. We're almost there. First, I wanna see how strong this thing is." He leaped to the top of the sphere with a pickaxe in hand and prepared to take a swing.

"Wait!" yelled Tommy, giving up his sanctuary. "You might wreck it."

"You!" hissed Mitch. He dropped the pickaxe and ran toward Tommy.

Wishing he were anywhere else, Tommy stood his ground, grateful that Mitch was empty-handed.

Muggie stepped in front of Tommy, protectively. "Leave him alone, Mitch."

"Stay out of this, *Mugly*," said Mitch as he pushed her aside.

Then someone yelled, "Back off!" and shoved Mitch hard. With a sinking feeling, Tommy realized he'd done it. For the second time that day, Mitch grabbed his shirt and brandished a fist.

Muggie wedged herself between them again. "Still planning to join the Army, Mitch? Because they won't let you in if you have a criminal record."

Mitch hesitated, seething. "Had to bring your girlfriend to protect you, eh, Steiber? Fine! We'll settle this later. Now get out of my woods!"

He let go of Tommy and went back to digging.

"They're not *your* woods," said Tommy tremulously, all the while thinking how much he loved Carrie Anne Muglyn. "And that's not your... thing." Mitch yelled more threats, which Tommy ignored. "Look, I think I know what it is. I think it's...a spaceship of some kind."

Tommy enjoyed three seconds of silence before they all started laughing.

"Seriously, guys," said Muggie, "it could be something dangerous. Just leave it alone, and we'll report it to the authorities."

Mitch pointed a finger at Muggie, and snarled, "Don't even think about it. It's mine."

"No, it's not," said Tommy. "It belonged to Cujo. He wasn't a dog. He was an alien, and I think this was his ship."

Chuckey was the only one not laughing this time. "Then why didn't he just fly it home?"

Scott stopped digging. "Maybe because his ship was stuck in the mud. He could've been caught in a mud slide when he landed."

"That's brilliant!" said Tommy.

"That's stupid," said Mitch. "A spaceship could easily break out of some mud."

Scott shook his head. "Not necessarily. The high iron content of this red clay could disable a spaceship's energy field, rendering it useless."

Muggie was still laughing. "So all you have to do is fish it out of the mud, and you'll have a working spaceship? You guys have been reading too many comic books."

Scott pulled a tape measure out of his backpack. "Theoretically, an energy field could support the entire sphere as long as more than half is unburied, which is about—"

Woooommmm! The sphere vibrated briefly as a wave of light rolled across its surface.

The boys scrambled out of the hole within seconds.

"It's a good thing that's just a theory," said Muggie, her voice shaking.

Woooommmm! The sphere vibrated again, though this time Tommy swore it moved. "Did you see that? I think it's trying to break free."

Woo-wooom! Woo-woom! Woo-woom!

Mitch grabbed the pickaxe, ready to strike the sphere. "I'm not letting my ship get away."

"Are you crazy?" yelled Tommy.

With a deep boom and blast of energy, the sphere wrenched itself free, knocking Tommy and the others off their feet.

Whatever You Do, Don't Touch It

Tommy looked up and saw a seamless orb floating just above the ground, aglow and humming steadily.

"Just for the record, Tommy," said Chuckey as they all got to their feet, "I believe you."

Mitch rubbed his hands together greedily. "Well, well, well. I got myself a spaceship." He reached out to touch it.

"Mitch, that could kill you!" warned Muggie.

Tommy shrugged. "Then again, give it a shot. Who knows?"

Mitch took a step back. "All right, Mr. *Space Expert*, how do I get inside my ship?"

"Look, it's Cujo's ship. *Cu-jo's*—hear the syllables! He was an alien, and I can prove it."

Reluctantly, Tommy led them to the tall pine under which Cujo was buried. However, when he dug into the hole, all he found was ash. "He was right here. I buried him just this morning."

With a glare, Mitch stepped close to Tommy. "Either way, the mutt's dead. My crew dug up the ship, so it belongs to me, Scott, and... Where's Chuckey?"

The chubby boy was gone.

Muggie stared at the sphere. "Don't tell me..."

Mitch tried his walkie-talkie. "Eagle One to Private Peats, come in."

"That won't do much good," said Scott, holding up Chuckey's radio. "What are the chances he's inside?"

Tommy stepped closer to the ship. "I wouldn't bet against it. Is it me, or is the ship bigger than it was?"

"It *does* look bigger," said Muggie, her face pinched with worry. "He's got to be in there."

Mitch clapped Scott's shoulder. "Looks like we have no choice. Salinas, go in after him."

Scott didn't budge. "I think I'd rather do pushups, sir."

"I'll do it," blurted Tommy, surprising himself.

"Just remember, it's *my* ship," warned Mitch. "So don't go flying off with it."

"You don't have to do this, Tommy," said Muggie, grabbing his hand.

Tommy's heart skipped a beat. "He's my friend. Besides, I need to know what's inside."

Slowly, he stepped forward, looking up at the shimmering globe. Its light looked oddly familiar. He reached up and touched it, feeling the warm metal beneath his fingertips for less than an instant.

The humming stopped, and the woods disappeared. Tommy found himself in an oval room that was undoubtedly the inside of the ship. Though the floor was flat, the walls and ceiling formed a semicircle. Soft light filled every part of the room, though Tommy couldn't tell where it came from. The walls were smooth and bare, except for a single door on the far wall.

A strange sound broke the silence. It seemed to come from the other side of the door. The door opened suddenly, and out came Chuckey.

"Hey, Tommy," he called casually. "Check out this bathroom."

"You nut! You went and touched the ship?"

"Yeah. I hope Mitch doesn't make me do more pushups. My arms are killing me."

With a flash of light, Scott suddenly appeared on the opposite side of the room. Something about his arrival left Tommy disoriented.

"Cool!" Scott looked around. "Did the room just get bigger? Because we saw the ship grow when Tommy disappeared."

"Yeah, it *is* bigger," said Tommy, realizing the change, and then he frowned at Scott. "Hold on. You left Muggie alone out there with Mitch?"

Chuckey patted Tommy's shoulder. "Don't worry. I never saw Mitch actually punch anyone... that hard."

"Really?" asked Tommy, looking around the cabin for an exit. "Because I seem to remember both of you being there the last time he beat her up." Scott and Chuckey managed to look guilty. "If we don't find a way out, Muggie will go for help, and Mitch will try to stop her."

"Sounds like a fight to me," said Scott, opening the only door in the room. "Is this a bathroom?"

"I hope so," said Chuckey, "or I just peed somewhere I shouldn't have."

There was another disorienting flash, and Muggie appeared in what was now an even larger room.

"Welcome aboard," said Tommy, relieved to see her. "We're trying to find an exit."

She paced the floor, arms folded and scowling. "I'm not in any hurry to get back out there. Mitch is a big jerk!"

Tommy's chest tightened. "What did he do?"

"Nothing," said Muggie, looking around. "Tommy, this is amazing. I'll never doubt you again." She planted a kiss on his cheek, leaving him lightheaded.

"Hey Muggie, check out the bathroom," said Chuckey. "Look! Now there are two!"

Tommy ran his hands along the cabin walls, feeling for a lever, a button, or even a seam. "There has to be a way out."

"You're looking for something mechanical," said Scott. "But I think it works on electromagnetics and matter-energy transformation. I'll bet the ship is controlled from this console."

Tommy turned to find Scott standing in front of what looked like a long, legless table sticking out of the wall at an angle. Dozens of raised symbols covered its surface. "Where did that come from?" Tommy asked, certain it hadn't been there before.

"Wow! Look at all the pictographs," exclaimed Muggie.

"Try that one," said Chuckey, touching a symbol that looked like a square with a corner missing.

Tommy shouted in warning. Luckily, nothing happened. "Stop touching things, Chuckey! That's what got us stuck in here to begin with."

Chuckey shrugged, and said, "I thought it looked like a door."

"Yeah, well you could've fired a photon torpedo and killed Captain Steelmaker," said Scott, "which I think would get you demoted...*again*."

"*Captain* Steelmaker?" Muggie's lip curled in disgust.

"You know he'll claim himself Captain of the ship the minute he gets in here." Scott stood back, folding his arms. "I'll vote for Tommy, of course, as long as it doesn't look like I'll get pounded."

"Me, too," said Chuckey. "I don't do well with personal injury."

Tommy studied the console's symbols. "I got a better idea. We figure out how to fly this thing and take off—*Flash*—without him." Tommy suddenly had a renewed respect for timing, as Mitch finally joined them.

Don't Try to Fly It, Stupid

"Without who?" asked Mitch from the other side of the room.

"Hey Mitch, check out the bathrooms," said Chuckey.

"Don't even think about flying this ball bearing without me," Mitch threatened as he walked up behind Tommy, "or I'll make sure you're the first thing on my *criminal record*."

Tommy hated to hate; it just wasn't healthy. But when it came to Mitch, he could easily leave the troll stranded on a distant planet. A smile came over him at the thought that maybe he'd get the chance.

"Mitch, you should've waited outside," said Tommy. "Now who's gonna go for help if we can't get out of here?"

"Danny knows where we are," Muggie announced, with a sharp glance at Mitch.

Mitch folded his arms, and smugly said, "I don't need any help. All I need is a captain's chair."

Before Mitch had finished his sentence, the floor under Tommy's feet buckled, and a padded chair popped up right under his butt. "See, my ship even listens to me. Now get out of my seat, Steiber."

"It's not your ship," said Tommy, unmoving.

"Obviously, I'm the Captain; I already have a crew. Ain't that right, men?" Mitch glared at Scott and Chuckey while cracking his knuckles. Both boys caved in immediately, pledging their support to Mitch.

"It was my dog...alien thing's ship," argued Tommy.

"I dug it up!" Mitch countered.

"There's an easy way to settle this," said Muggie. "Whichever one of you two figures out how to exit the ship gets to be the Captain."

"Done!" said Mitch, shoving Tommy out of the captain's chair. "You already had a try, loser."

"Hey!" complained Tommy. "Don't just start–" Mitch was already touching symbols haphazardly, though nothing happened. Tommy felt the underside of the console for a switch. "It's like it's not turned on."

Mitch jumped out of the chair. "What am I thinking? The ship follows my orders. This'll be easy." He tried several short commands, including *exit*, *open door*, and *leave ship*, but the vessel didn't respond.

While Mitch tried more phrases, Tommy went back to the captain's chair.

"You can do it, Tommy," Muggie whispered as she squeezed in beside him.

Tommy shook his head. "This was Cujo's ship. I don't know how it works."

"Well, what would *he* do, bark at it?" she asked with a chuckle.

"No, he never barked. He howled..." A jolt of excitement whipped through Tommy's body. "No, he sang!"

Could it be that simple? All those times Cujo had been hungry, or wanted to go out, or just wanted Tommy's attention, he would always howl the same song: a handful of sweet notes that Tommy could never forget.

Ever so softly, Tommy sang the notes that made up Cujo's signature howl. Instantly, the melody resonated from the console and some of the symbols glowed with a steady blue light.

"Wow, Tommy! How'd you do that?" asked Chuckey, while Muggie clapped in excitement.

"My turn to try again," said Mitch, giving Tommy a shove.

While he still had the chance, Tommy sang a soft note and touched one of the symbols. The vessel shuddered with a deep thud, and the room filled with daylight. All along the center of the wall, a horizontal strip several feet wide became transparent, like glass.

"Score!" exclaimed Chuckey. "Maybe that's a way out!"

"Lucky guess," said Mitch sullenly.

Scott knocked on the window. "It's solid. Uh, Muggie, your little brother's out there."

Standing beyond the glass, little Danny Muglyn eyed the vessel curiously.

"No, Danny!" shouted Muggie, waving her arms. "Go home! Go for help!"

Danny stepped closer to the ship, reaching his hand out tentatively, oblivious to his sister's cries.

The room expanded with a familiar flash. "Wow!" cried Danny. "I knew I'd find you guys in here. What is this, a spaceship?"

"Don't get your hopes up, kiddo," said Muggie. "We don't know what it is just...yet. What's that sound?"

Tommy heard it, too. It was a low, thrumming vibration beneath the floor. With every second, it grew higher in pitch.

"What button did you push, Steiber?" demanded Mitch anxiously.

Tommy looked closer at the symbol he'd touched, swallowing hard. It pictured a small circle moving away from a larger one. To his horror, all of the other symbols went dark. For once, he feared something worse than Mitch Steelmaker. "We gotta get out of here!" he shouted as the sound grew shrill. He ran to the window, expecting the worst.

"Make it stop!" cried Mitch, pounding the console with his fists.

All at once the ship went silent, except for a soft hum. Tommy exhaled sharply, though his relief didn't last. He felt movement, like riding an elevator up to the top floor of a tall building—except this elevator kept moving faster and faster.

"Here we go!" said Danny gleefully.

Tommy watched Deep Creek Woods, the gorge, and his neighborhood fall away.

Don't Get Eaten

Earth quickly shrank as the ship's speed increased. Bright stars amid black space filled the panoramic window.

Mitch ran into one of the bathrooms and threw up, giving Tommy something to be happy about. Tommy staggered back to the captain's chair, his head spinning. The rest of the passengers, looking rather sickly, slumped down onto wide, padded seats that had emerged from the cabin walls.

"I feel awful," breathed Muggie.

"The ship's artificial gravity must be making us weak," said Scott. When the others gave him a queer look, he responded, "Better that than all of us flying around weightless. Hopefully, we'll get used to it."

A pale and anxious-looking Mitch emerged from the bathroom. "Status report, Lieutenant," he managed to say.

Scott gave a weak salute. "We're trapped in an alien spaceship, hurtling through the solar system, Captain."

Mitch made a beeline for Tommy. "Get this silver bullet turned around, or I swear, I'll knock you to the moon."

"Too late," said Chuckey as the moon flew past the window.

"I'm trying!" insisted Tommy, though he truly didn't know what to do. He touched every symbol on the console, singing all the while, but the ship just went faster and faster and faster.

"Mitch is right," said Muggie, though she didn't look happy admitting it. "We could die out here."

Tommy threw his hands up, and wailed, "I can't stop it. I think it's on autopilot."

"No, you guys, we have to keep going," insisted Danny. "Don't you see? This is all part of the story. The Space Elves need our help. We're on a mission!"

"Someone shut that kid up," said Mitch.

"Danny's right," said Chuckey. "It's like this is right out of one of Tommy's comic books!"

Mitch opened his mouth to reprimand his soldier, but ran back to the bathroom instead.

"But this isn't in any of my comic books," Tommy protested, looking around the ship.

"There has to be a connection to the Loremaster saga," said Muggie. She blushed. "Okay, I've read a few...only when Danny leaves them lying around. But I don't really understand what's going on. Why are the Space Elves fighting robots?"

"Doom Droids!" said Chuckey and Danny at once.

"Much deadlier than robots," added Scott.

Tommy explained that the Space Elves had battled their archenemies, the Galactic Goblins, for ages, with victories and defeats on both sides. Not long ago, however, the Goblins took the upper hand, destroyed the Elven defenses, and wiped out nearly all of the Elves. In desperation, the Elves invented droids that could fight in their place. They were the Doom Droids. The Droids succeeded in fighting back the Goblins and dealt the fiends one crushing blow after another until, like the Elves, the Goblins were nearly annihilated.

With their victory against the Goblins secured, the Elves tried to terminate their

Android Defense Program, but the Droids had other plans.

"And then what happened?" asked Muggie, wide-eyed.

"That's what we're waiting to find out in the next issue, number thirteen," said Chuckey as he looked at Tommy with anticipation.

"I haven't been able to finish it. Every time I try, it always ends up bad for the Elves. Seriously, how do you stop Doom Droids? They're stronger; they're faster; and they're always one step ahead with technology."

"Tommy, what happens in issue thirteen?" asked Muggie.

Tommy cringed. "The Doom Droids turn their aggression against their creators. Their programming won't allow them to kill the Elves, but they become masters at capturing them. Soon, all but a few Elves are imprisoned on

Grenatia, the Elven home world. There, the Elven race is encased in crystallox, sealed away...forever."

"That's it?" asked an incredulous Mitch, his head sticking out of the bathroom. "That's how your story ends?" All he got from Tommy and the others was stunned silence. "What? I was listening."

Tommy walked to the window. "It doesn't matter anyway. My stories don't have anything to do with a small spaceship on Earth."

"Tommy, where did you get the idea for your comic books?" asked Muggie.

"The stories just sort of came to me, in dreams, usually. It started around two years ago, right about the time we all stopped hanging out." Tommy caught himself glancing at Mitch angrily.

"Wasn't that when you found Cujo?" Chuckey wondered.

"To the day," said Tommy, his stomach tingling with excitement. Maybe there was a connection! For an instant, he was back in the woods that night, surrounded by holes, with Cujo reaching out to him. Flashes of color revealed noble Space Elves overrun by Goblins and Droids. There was something more; something bright...

"You know, this *could* be part of the story," said Scott, pondering the idea. "If the Silver Bullet really was Cujo's ship, maybe he was on his way to help the Elves when he got stuck on Earth."

"The Silver Bullet?" asked Chuckey.

"Well, the ship needs a name," explained Scott.

"How can one alien rescue the Space Elves from an army of Doom Droids?" Tommy wondered aloud. Before he finished the question,

Tommy knew the answer. "He'd have to be a Loremaster!"

"Wow!" shouted Danny. "Cujo was a Loremaster? I thought he was just an ugly dog with stinky breath."

"But even a Loremaster would need help." Tommy exhaled long and slow. Hunger gnawed at his stomach, and his eyelids wanted to close. "I don't know, guys. I still don't see how it all fits together."

"That's because you have to finish the story," said Muggie encouragingly.

Chuckey's eyes widened. "Yeah, Tommy! What happens *after* issue thirteen?

"Look, they're not even my stories, apparently. I must have gotten them from Cujo somehow. I don't know what happens next; I don't know how to save the Elves; and I don't know how to get us back home."

Frustrated by the dead end and his friends' incessant questions, Tommy retreated to the only vomit-free bathroom on the ship. When he came out later, Scott was pulling granola bars and bottles of water from his backpack and handing them out. The snacks lifted everyone's spirits, including Tommy's.

"I just wish I knew where we're headed," he said, sitting down in the captain's chair. As if the ship had understood his request, an electronic chart appeared on the wall above the console. It showed hundreds of stars in constellations Tommy had never seen, and language and symbols he couldn't read.

"Well, I guess you're not the only one who commands the ship," Muggie bragged to Mitch, who was seated on the floor next to the bathroom. The older boy returned a glare that quickly shifted to Tommy. Tommy turned away, wishing he could eject Mitch into space. He looked for a symbol on the console that might do the trick.

"That must be us," said Scott, pointing to a tiny blinking dot moving across the space map. The dot was approaching a small, purple symbol on the screen. Looking closer, Tommy thought it resembled a spider web.

"Why does that make me nervous?" he asked, looking out the window.

Everyone seemed to see it at once—a collection of huge reflective shapes scattered in the space before them like the shattered pieces of a giant mirror. Before anyone had a chance to ask what the shapes were, a network of bright purple lines lit up, connecting them. The lines formed an irregular polygon with seven sides and seven angles.

"Awesome heptagon," said Scott. "You don't see those very often."

Other lines crisscrossed the interior of the shape, forming a web. With a flash of light, the web collapsed, leaving a lavender tunnel that spun away.

"That's definitely not in any of my stories," said Tommy.

"But if it was, what would it do?" asked Muggie.

"Take us to another part of the galaxy, I guess...to the Grenatian solar system, where the Elves live."

"Like a shortcut?" asked Danny.

Scott snapped his fingers. "Of course. Otherwise, it would take years, even centuries, to get there."

"We better hope that's what it is," groaned Mitch as they neared the tunnel.

Danny looked at Tommy, suddenly anxious. Tommy held his hand. "It's all part of the story, right Dan Man?" Danny nodded, forcing a smile.

Tommy felt someone clasp his other hand. Muggie smiled, squeezing his fingers.

The ship slowed down and nearly stopped as it entered the tunnel. Then it swooped into the opening with a burst of speed. Tommy's stomach flipped over like he was riding a roller coaster. An instant later, the tunnel vanished and normal space returned. The passengers *woohooed* and wanted to ride again, everyone except Mitch, of course. The soldier-wannabe still hadn't found his space legs.

"Looks like you were right, Tommy," said Scott, pointing to the space map. It looked drastically different than before.

"Are we there yet?" whined Chuckey.

"How should I know?" said Tommy through a yawn. As the others chatted, he laid down on one of the seats and stretched. Forcing his eyes to stay open, he looked out the window at the sea of stars, noticing their beauty for the first time. This was where Cujo would have been if only the Loremaster had lived another day. But they were here in his place, completing his mission. Yet, what were they supposed to do?

Trusting the Silver Bullet to keep them safe for now, Tommy let his eyelids close.

* * *

"Wake up!" shouted an excited Chuckey as he shook Tommy's shoulder. "Mitch and Scott are already outside."

Struggling to remember where he was, Tommy pushed himself up. The ship was still and silent. An ice-colored light filled the window. "We landed?" cried Tommy, startling Muggie awake. "We landed!" He looked around for Chuckey, but the boy was gone.

"Where are we?" asked a dazed Muggie.

"I don't know," puzzled Tommy, gazing out the window, "but it looks amazing." He saw a moonlike place under a black sky packed with stars. Ponds and lakes of glowing water dotted the landscape and filled the air with eerie light. Not too far away, Mitch and Scott were hiking up a small hill, and Chuckey was jogging toward them.

"They're crazy!" said Muggie, looking outside. "The atmosphere could be toxic."

"How did they get outside?" asked Danny, bursting out of the bathroom while zipping up his pants. "Hey you guys!" he hollered, smacking his hand on the window. "Wait for—" Muggie screamed when Danny suddenly appeared outside, already running after the other boys.

"Wait, Danny!" she cried, pressing her hands against the window. An instant later, she was outside, looking shocked.

Tommy put his hand on the window and imagined leaving the ship. He blinked and found himself outside, surrounded by warm air that smelled like a desert. He and Muggie quickly caught up to the others at the top of the hill. The boys stood motionless, all staring in the same direction.

"Unbelievable," whispered Tommy, when his eyes found the wreckage of a crashed ship in the distance. The only thing more amazing than seeing the huge vessel before him was that it looked exactly like the Elven ships he'd drawn for his comic books. It had a sleek, green metal hull, and twin fusion engines, with black stabilizer fins.

"They're shipwrecked! Of course! The Doom Droids haven't captured *all* the Elves. *These* Elves must have been on their way to Grenatia to rescue their people when they crashed here. C'mon!" Tommy headed toward the crash site, motioning for the others to follow him.

"Hold it, Steiber," ordered Mitch. "This is my landing party."

"Would you stop the military crap?" asked Tommy, rolling his eyes and immediately wishing he hadn't.

Mitch stormed up to him as usual. "Don't be a sore loser, Steiber. I found a way off the

Silver Bullet, which makes me Captain. Either follow my orders or go back to the ship."

Tommy's comfort level with Mitch up close and threatening hadn't changed. He waited, hoping someone else would object. After all, it was *his* ship, not Mitch's. "Fine! What do you wanna do?"

Ignoring the question, Mitch ordered Scott and Chuckey to scout ahead. After testing their radios, the boys marched down the hill toward the wreckage, fanning out as they went.

"At least they'll be the first to get eaten if we run into hostile aliens," joked Danny.

Scott reported seeing more rocks and glowing ponds, as well as strange purple shrubs. Chuckey reported that he was hungry. Finally, Mitch gave the order to move out.

As they approached the ship, it became clear that it had skidded a short distance and ended up in the middle of a small lake. Strangely enough, it rested on top of the water. Tommy realized that the lake was frozen.

"It looks solid," said Scott, squatting next to the edge of the lake.

Mitch stomped on the surface with the heel of his hiking boot. The ice didn't budge. "Let's go," he ordered, leading the way across the lake.

"Ice, with these temperatures?" Tommy wondered aloud. "Maybe crossing *Shipwreck Lake* isn't such a good idea."

Muggie caught up to Mitch, tiptoeing over the ice. "Mitch, why don't we try calling out to the ship first to see if anyone—"

"Or anything!" interjected Scott.

"—is in there," finished Muggie.

"Yo, alien vessel!" hollered Mitch as he walked, his voice echoing. "Anyone aboard?'

The ship was as silent as it had been before. "Good. That means any treasure on board is mine."

Immediately Mitch and his boys started speculating about what they'd find on the ship. Tommy, however, was looking down through the ice, where he swore he saw something move.

"Did you see that?" he asked Muggie as a long, thick shape glided far below. "There's something down there, guys; something big. I think it's a snake."

Mitch froze in place and then slowly turned around. "Very funny, Steiber," he fumed through clenched teeth.

"I see it, too," said Chuckey, pointing down.

"Retreat!" screamed Mitch, racing for the shore.

As they ran, Tommy saw the shape under the ice grow rapidly. "It's coming up. Get out of the way!"

A giant, horned serpent popped up through the ice like it was water. Its jaws barely missed Tommy as he rolled away. The beast rose straight into the air, roaring at the stars. Then it fell back down, disappearing through the ice.

Tommy scrambled to his feet and ran toward the others on shore before stopping a moment later. They were all safe, except for Danny. The younger boy was still out on the lake, frozen with fear.

"Danny!" shrieked Muggie, sprinting back onto the ice.

"Stop!" yelled Tommy. "Don't move. I think that's what makes it attack."

Muggie slid to a halt, stricken. "You'd better be right about this, Steiber."

Everyone waited. Shipwreck Lake was silent, except for the sound of their labored breathing.

Tommy walked toward Danny as slow as he could. Under the ice he saw two figures moving, and then three. With every step there seemed to be more.

Danny saw them too. "Tommy," he said, shaking all over, "in the story, do I get eaten?"

"No, kiddo, you stay very, very still."

Danny shook his head as tears rolled down his face.

Tommy dared walking faster. *Bad idea*, he thought as a dark shape rushed to the surface.

The serpent burst out of the lake. It snagged Tommy's sneaker on its horn, lifting him up by his ankle. He wriggled out of his shoe, landing hard on the ice. Beneath him, another shape emerged. Tommy tried to get to his feet, but his shoeless foot kept slipping.

Roaring as it came up, the scaled beast missed him. It cocked its head sideways to catch him as it came back down. Danny slammed into Tommy, knocking him out from under the serpent's gaping maw as it fell through the ice.

Before he knew it, Tommy was on his feet, running with Danny under his arm. Dozens of shapes slithered wildly beneath the surface. "This is definitely not in the story," he muttered, expecting to die at any moment.

"Run zigzag, Steiber, *zigzag!*" he heard Mitch yell.

Tommy immediately followed orders, changing course every few steps. It worked. Serpents erupted through the ice on either side, always just missing him.

Finally, Tommy leaped onto the shore, and they tumbled to the ground. He laid still for several moments, feeling his pounding heart in his chest and the heavenly soil beneath his body.

Muggie clung to her brother, rocking him as he wept into her shoulder. Scott and Chucky hugged Danny, too, while Mitch extended a hand to help Tommy up.

Tommy looked back at the placid surface of the lake. Although grateful that he'd lost only a shoe, he hated to admit something. "Thank you, Captain," he said as Mitch pulled him to his feet. "You just saved our lives."

Avoid Getting Pulverized

Rocks crunched under their shoes as the six circumvented Shipwreck Lake. In Tommy's case, it was one shoe and a dirty sock. Muggie had insisted that they return to the ship, but the boys, even Danny, wanted to keep exploring.

Tommy promised himself that he'd stop Mitch from putting them in danger again, though he wasn't quite sure how he'd do it. Mitch had Scott and Chuckey trained to do whatever he said, and he always said the opposite of whatever Tommy wanted. Bullies had to be some of the most unmanageable people in the world.

With the Elven ship inaccessible, Mitch decided to look for survivors in the surrounding area. Not far from the crash site, they came upon a gruesome scene. Dozens of skeletons littered a makeshift camp.

"Oh, no!" Tommy sat down on a rock, unable to move. These were the last of the free Space Elves. Only bones wrapped in green body armor remained.

"What happened to them?" Muggie wondered, her eyes bright with tears.

"It doesn't look like there was a battle,' Scott said softly.

"They were marooned," Mitch suggested. "They ran out of supplies and starved to death."

"No wonder Cujo was always digging near the gorge," said Muggie, her voice thick. "He must have known they were stranded. He never gave up trying to save them."

Danny leaned into his sister for comfort. "Tommy, maybe that's why he sent you those stories in your dreams."

Tommy's heart wrenched with pain. "And all I did was turn them into stupid comic books. I've ruined everything." He put his head in his hands.

"Maybe it's not too late," said Chuckey.

"No, I think they're pretty much permanently dead, Chuck," said Tommy irritably.

"Not these guys," insisted Chuckey. "The Elves on Grenatia. We can save *them*."

"Look, they were the elite Elven Guard," said Tommy, pointing to the insignia on the armor—a flourishing oak tree crossed by a gold lightning bolt. "Even with the help of a Loremaster, I don't see how they could've rescued thousands of imprisoned Elves from the Doom Droids. And if *they* couldn't do it, we don't stand a chance. We'd either get captured or killed."

"But Tommy," whispered Danny, teary eyed.

"It's over, Dan Man. We came all this way for nothing. End of story. We should just go home before we end up like these poor guys."

No one moved or said anything for a while. Then Mitch started rummaging around the campsite. He tossed a pair of silver boots to Tommy.

"Leave 'em alone, Mitch," demanded Tommy, his blood hot. "They deserve to be treated with respect."

Mitch continued stripping equipment from the corpses. "They're dead, Steiber. I need the armor and weapons to protect my troops."

"No, you don't. We're leaving, l*eav-ing*—hear the syllables."

Mitch gave Chuckey a helmet. "I'm not going home empty-handed. With weapons and armor, we can kill those snake monsters and get to the shipwreck. And who knows what else is around here." He handed Scott something that looked like a laser rifle.

"Mitch, you can't give them guns," insisted Muggie. "It's too dangerous. And don't you start," she added to Danny, who had picked up a shield.

"C'mon, Carrie Anne," complained Danny when she took it away. "It was just lying there."

Tommy clenched his hands. "Captain, or not, there's no way I'm letting you risk our lives again, Mitch."

"Risk our lives? That's what you did by bringing us here and getting us caught up in your little space adventure. I'm just making it all worth the trouble. Me and my men are gonna find some treasure, Steiber, and there's nothing you can do about it."

Mitch turned his attention to the laser rifle in his hand. "All I have to do is figure out how this thing–" *Zap!*

A bolt of red energy shot out of the gun, blasting Muggie off her feet. She landed on her back, unconscious.

"MUGGIE!" Disbelief blurred Tommy's vision. He collapsed to the ground at Muggie's side. She wasn't breathing. "Don't die like this, Muggie. We have to get you home. Please don't die!"

"I'll start CPR," said Scott. But before he could put his hands to Muggie's chest, her eyes opened, and she inhaled sharply.

"Oh, Carrie Anne," cried Danny, hugging his sister. He buried his face in her hair, bawling.

"I'm okay," she whispered, trying to pat him.

Mitch laughed casually. "It's a good thing you were holding that shield, or you would've been toast."

Tommy saw red.

His body launched itself at Mitch Steelmaker. His hands turned to fists, swinging and striking. He heard himself screaming and cursing. Others shouted. Then the world spun completely around, and he landed on his back with a *thump*.

Tommy clambered to his feet, ignoring the shouts. Mitch stood up slowly, all covered in dust, and with blood dripping from his lip and nose.

Tommy fought to hide a smile of satisfaction before reality set in. Realizing what he'd done, he tried to speak, to somehow talk his way out of it, but his lungs couldn't keep air.

Mitch touched his lip, and looked at his bloody fingertips with curiosity. Then he nodded, smiling wickedly, eyes fixed on Tommy. It was a look that said, "This is it, Steiber."

Every muscle in Tommy's body turned to wet pasta. Starry specks flickered around his eyes. His arms felt like two sausages as he lifted them to defend himself.

Mitch took a huge swing at his stomach. Tommy tried to block the punch. It never came. Instead, a rock hard fist slammed into his face. The ground came up behind him, hitting him hard. Then the sky, so full of stars, turned completely black.

Don't Feed the Monsters

"I won't let you do it," vowed Muggie.

Mitch ignored her. He held the firecracker before the turtle's snout, taunting it.

"Careful, Mitch," warned Chuckey. "Them things can nip off your finger faster than lightning."

Tommy silently wagered his next ten birthday wishes hoping lightning would strike.

The snapper took the bait.

"Lighter," ordered Mitch.

Scott unzipped one of his backpack's pockets.

"Don't give it to him, Scott," said Muggie.

Scott tossed Mitch the lighter. He looked at Muggie and shrugged. It was his way of saying, "If I don't give it to him, he'll just take it."

Flicking the lighter, Mitch held the flame to the fuse. Muggie pushed him aside and yanked the fuse out of the firecracker.

"What are ya doing?" cried Mitch. "You saw how long it took me to get him to bite that." He turned to Scott. "Give me another firecracker. Out of the way, Mugly."

Muggie refused to budge. "You're not hurting this turtle." Faster than a snapper's bite, she snatched the lighter out of Mitch's hand and pitched it into the woods.

Mitch responded with a curse and a brutal punch to her stomach.

"Leave her alone, you big jerk!" screamed Tommy.

"You want some of this, too, Steiber?" asked Mitch, stalking toward him. He pulled back

for a swing, but Muggie tackled him. Mitch came out on top and landed several more punches before the boys pulled him off.

Muggie rose, with tears and blood streaming down her face. She took off. Tommy followed, but couldn't catch her. Each step grew heavier with guilt. He was to blame. He was the one who'd found the turtle.

A firecracker exploded, echoing through the woods.

* * *

Tommy woke up. Through one eye he saw that the stars had returned to the sky. He wondered which one was home. His head tinged with pain when he blinked. It throbbed when he tried to get up.

"Stay there," Muggie commanded, and put a warm hand to his chest. "Let me take a look at you." She lifted a wet cloth from his eye. "It looks like the bleeding stopped."

"You got a black eye," Danny informed him, almost enviously. "But you should see—"

"Danny, I thought you were supposed to be keeping a lookout for hostile aliens," said Muggie.

Danny saluted her, saying "Aye, aye, sister." Then he climbed to the top of some nearby boulders, and scanned the area.

Muggie turned back to Tommy. She brushed his hair away from his swollen eye. "Thanks for sticking up for me." Her voice was as soft as her fingertips.

He swallowed. "When Mitch shot you, I thought…"

"It just knocked the wind out of me. Anyway, I worked things out with Mitch. He's not gonna be pushing anyone around any more."

"How did you manage that?"

"Chuckey's coming back," shouted Danny as he leapt down from the rocks.

"Back from where?" asked Tommy, sitting up.

"They went exploring," Danny sulked, "and Carrie Anne wouldn't let me go."

Muggie rolled her eyes. "I don't know about you, but I'm ready to go home. I need a good meal and a hot shower. Can you imagine how worried our parents are right now?"

"I know." Tommy thought about Mom, and he remembered how disappointed she'd been with him.

Chuckey ran into camp, out of breath. He looked formidable in his Elven body armor, though the helmet didn't fit, and the laser rifle seemed dangerously out of place.

He ripped open Scott's backpack and started rummaging through it. "We found some treasure, you guys," he said, pausing for several big breaths, "in a cave back that way."

"What do you mean, treasure?" Muggie asked.

"Something golden, but we can't get to it 'cause this monster's in the way. We're gonna try and blow it up."

"Monster?" cried Danny, grabbing Muggie's hand.

"Private Peats, report!" ordered Mitch over Chuckey's walkie-talkie.

"I can't find the firecrackers, sir," Chuckey whined into his radio. He slung the backpack over his shoulder. "I'll just bring the whole thing."

Tommy felt his tender eye. "You've *got* to be kidding me, Chuckey. Firecrackers?"

"Well, the monster's too quick for blasters. We miss every time."

"Treasure or no treasure, we're leaving," said Muggie. She grabbed Chuckey's radio. "Mitch, it's time to go."

"I'm not talking to you; you broke my arm!" was Mitch's reply.

Tommy gaped at her. "You did what?"

"It's probably just a fracture," she said with a smirk. "What do you think I've been doing these past two years?" She faked a karate kick to his head.

"It was great," said Chuckey. "You should see *his* black eye. After Mitch knocked you out, she evened the score."

"For both of us," added Muggie.

Danny tugged his sister's arm. "C'mon, Carrie Anne, I wanna see the treasure."

Grudgingly, Tommy donned the boots Mitch had picked out for him. Then he hiked with the others a short way to the cave entrance. A tall rock arch led down to a huge underground cavern. A large pond, like the ones on the planet's surface, filled most of the interior. Mitch and Scott stood near the pond's edge.

"Hey Steiber, you feeling better?" called Mitch, his legs and chest armored, and his arm in a sling. "I seriously didn't mean to hit you that hard, man."

"We won't be doing any more hitting, will we, Mitch?" declared Muggie.

Mitch scowled. "I said I'm not talking to you."

"Don't be a sore loser," she bantered.

"I didn't lose. You broke my arm. How do you expect me to fight?"

Tommy barely heard their squabbling. A bright light far across the pond called to him like a beacon. Its golden color could only be one thing: the Elf of Light. He had refused to believe in her, even forgotten her, but there she was.

Someone grabbed Tommy's arm, yanking him backwards. He was suddenly aware that he was several steps onto the ice.

Scott's grip was firm. "Where ya going, Tommy? There's another big snake out there. It's not as bad as the ones in Shipwreck Lake, but you'd better not take any chances."

"What is it, Tommy?" asked Muggie.

"It's her, the Elf of Light."

Chuckey frowned in confusion. "The who of what?"

"It's treasure," declared Mitch. "And as soon as we blow up that snake, we're gonna get it. Where are those firecrackers, Lieutenant?"

"She's a treasure, all right," said Tommy. "To the Elves, Angel's the most precious thing in the universe."

"Angels?" Muggie echoed. "Tommy, you're not making any sense."

A pink, worm-like creature stuck its head out of the ice, and stared at them with tiny, black eyes. It disappeared when Mitch lifted his rifle.

"Okay, we're only gonna get one shot at this," announced Mitch. "Peats, you go out onto the ice and get it to chase you. Then we'll–"

Tommy grabbed all of the remaining granola bars from Scott's backpack and walked onto the ice. He ignored everyone's questions and scanned the depths for movement. Just as he'd hoped, there was only one shape approaching. The pink creature emerged several yards in front of him.

"Are you hungry, little guy?" Tommy asked, unwrapping a granola bar and waving it back and forth. The worm followed his movements. "I hope you like health food." He threw the bar to one side. When the worm moved to get the snack, he sprinted for the far shore.

Halfway across the pond, the creature reappeared in front of him, bobbing up and down with anticipation. Tommy slid to a stop and opened another package.

"You got yourself one tame little worm," called Chuckey. "Do you see any others?"

"No. I think it's safe to cross."

Footsteps echoed through the cavern as the group jogged across the pond. The worm dipped back under the ice at the sound.

"It's okay, Wormy," said Tommy. "Here, go get it!" He tossed the bar away.

Hungry himself, Tommy gobbled down one of the granola bars as he ran to the shore with the others. Chuckey spied him stuffing the last two snacks into his pocket. "Those are for getting back," said Tommy, licking his lips.

Danny tapped Tommy's arm. "I think something's wrong with Wormy."

Looking back onto the pond, Tommy saw the creature shoot up out of the ice, convulsing and changing color rapidly. "Please tell me what I think is happening isn't really happening."

"Looks like a type of metamorphosis brought on by the consumption of nutrients," explained Scott. "Way to go, dude."

"How are we gonna get back?" asked Muggie.

Mitch answered her question by firing his laser rifle at the wiggling worm a dozen times. It writhed and whined in agony before disappearing through the ice.

Mitch shrugged when they all stared at him, horrified. "I can't stand snakes."

"But that was Wormy!" complained Danny.

Tommy clasped the little boy's shoulder. "Yes, Wormy, son of Serpent, who almost ate you."

Danny's eyes widened. "Oh...right. Hey Mitch, are you sure it's dead?"

Don't Trust the Aliens

Things were very different on the far side of the cavern. A frozen waterfall tumbled out of the ceiling, down the wall, and meandered as a stream of ice toward the pond. There, trapped inside a wall of ice, stood a beautiful female Elf, radiating golden light. She looked just like Tommy had drawn her. She had soft features and tiny pointed ears, with skin and hair the color of the setting sun.

"Is she...naked?" breathed Chuckey.

"Uh, looks like it," said Muggie. "It's a good thing that ice isn't crystal clear. Stop staring!"

"I know why she's naked," said Tommy, reaching out to touch the ice. It felt hard at first, but then it gave way beneath his fingers like soft dough. "Only living tissue can pass through this stuff. That's how Wormy and the serpents can swim through it."

"Wormy and the serpents," mused Chuckey. "That sounds like the name of a rock-n-roll band."

Tommy pushed further into the ice, reaching for Angel. A cold, burning sensation penetrated his skin, like dipping his arm in ice cold soda. He was in up to his shoulder, but not even close to her, and his shirt sleeve had caught on the surface. He pulled his arm out, grunting against the pain.

"She's in too deep," he said, taking off his shirt.

"You're not going in there, are you?" asked an incredulous Muggie. "Tommy, you could get frost bite. You could get stuck in there!"

Mitch tapped the ice with his rifle. "What's she doing in there, anyway?"

"She's in hibernation," Scott guessed, looking to Tommy for confirmation.

"She's the one the Elven Guard protected," Tommy explained. "Don't you guys get it?"

"Not really," said Chuckey.

Danny tugged Tommy's hand. "Tommy, finish the story."

Tommy sighed, unable to take his eyes off Angel. "Only one could save them. Legend told of special Elves long ago with extraordinary powers. These Elves of Light were believed to come in times of need. One such Elf was born recently, and her presence was kept secret. She and her protectors had embarked on a mission to free their people when their ship was ambushed by Goblins. They were so close to their goal, yet marooned on a dead planet. Angel called out to the Loremasters for help. Cujo heard her cry from across the galaxy, but he, too, was marooned."

"So, she's been waiting all this time?" asked Muggie, dipping her fingers into the ice. "I hope we're not too late."

Mitch clapped Tommy on the back. "Well, get in there, soldier."

Suddenly nauseous, Tommy realized that he would have to live his second greatest fear. It felt totally unfair, given the day he'd had so far. Stripping down to his boxers in the boys' locker room was bad enough. Now this? Yet, it was the only way to enter the ice, and the only way to save Angel. "I'm gonna need some privacy, guys," he said as he undressed.

The others turned away, muttering awkwardly. Scott pulled a flat orange square out of his backpack and unfolded it, producing a long rain poncho. He handed it to Muggie. "Just in case Angel's modest."

"Do you have another color?" asked Muggie. "This *really* clashes with gold."

"Uh oh," said Chuckey, pointing to the pond. "I think Wormy's back."

The worm, now a serpent, glided along the top of the ice, moving toward them. Mitch and his men fired at the giant snake repeatedly. Every time they hit their target it roared in anger.

"Hurry Tommy!" cried Muggie.

Taking a deep breath, Tommy stepped into the icy hot wall, pushing past the pain. With a second step, his entire body plunged into the ice. Unwilling to open his eyes, he reached, groping, and found Angel's wrist. He backed out, pulling her with him, but she was hard to move, and he had no leverage. It was like walking along the bottom of a swimming pool. His muscles went numb. His lungs ached for air. Consciousness faded.

Then a muscular arm wrapped around Tommy's waist, yanking him backwards. He clamped down on Angel's hand, and pulled with all the strength he had left. Warm air swept into his lungs as he, Mitch, and Angel fell to the ground. He opened his eyes when someone covered him with his sweatshirt. Everything was blurry chaos. The serpent roared, and the lasers fired.

"Take that, Wormy!" Danny yelled as he blasted the serpent. Scott shot at it, too, but the beast kept coming closer, slithering up the stream.

Too cold to move, Tommy's gaze came into focus on the rows of pointy teeth lining the serpent's mouth. They were all going to die; Angel, too, and all because of him.

Suddenly the beast clamped its jaws shut and began swaying back and forth as if entranced. Below it, Chuckey waved a granola bar. "Go get it, Wormy!" he shouted, hurling the snack out over the pond. The serpent turned and slithered away.

"She's waking up," said Muggie.

The Elf of Light stirred under the orange poncho. Her eyelids flickered open, and her breathing quickened. An anxious look filled her features.

"You're g-going to be okay," Tommy assured her through chattering teeth. Angel's sunflower eyes found his, and she almost smiled.

"Move out, people," ordered Mitch, "before that thing comes back."

Startled by his stern voice, Angel's gaze shifted to Mitch. Her chest heaved several times. Her body's light grew dim, and she shuddered. Then her golden glow exploded with energy, scattering her onlookers.

Tommy's body slammed back down to the ground, jarring the air from his lungs. He rolled over as Angel scuttled away. She ran onto the ice, stumbling every few steps. She was easy prey for an angry serpent. Breathless, Tommy screamed inside, reaching out to her with his thoughts.

Angel stopped and turned, her eyes burning into him from across the cavern pond. She started sinking into the ice just as Wormy sprouted up before her, roaring. Tommy stared in helpless frustration. No laser rifle or snack food could save her now.

Another blast of energy exploded from the Elf of Light.

Tommy braced against the force that struck him. When he looked again, Angel had reached the far shore. She'd left a lifeless serpent and a deep depression in the center of the pond.

"What just happened?" asked Chuckey, sitting up and straightening his helmet.

Mitch stood, nursing his broken arm. "She's gonna pay for that."

"She's just frightened, Mitch," said Muggie, rubbing her hip. "Let her go."

"No!" cried Tommy as Angel disappeared through the cavern opening. "We have to stop her. She's headed for the ship. She's leaving!"

Everyone clambered, stumbled, and ran after Angel. Mitch led the posse, with his laser rifle in hand.

"Don't shoot her, Mitch!" hollered Tommy, pulling on his clothes. By the time he'd caught up to them, they were watching the Silver Bullet lift off from across Shipwreck Lake. Mitch shot at it several times, with no effect.

"Great! That's just great, Mitch," complained Tommy. "Now she's gonna think we're her enemies."

"You got a better idea, Steiber? Because if you haven't noticed, now we're the ones who are marooned."

"You'd think she could have at least taken us along for the ride," said Chuckey dejectedly.

Tommy closed his eyes, seeing Angel's face in his mind. *Please don't leave us. We need you.* He scanned the night sky. A pair of lavender moons rose above the horizon. A shooting star streaked through the constellations, but there was no sign of the Silver Bullet.

* * *

Hours passed as they waited for some sign of Angel. Tommy tried calling out to her again and again with his thoughts. Whatever connection he thought he'd made with her in the cavern must have been his imagination.

The group shared the last granola bar while estimating how many days they could survive on the planet and contemplating whether or not the lake serpents were edible. Every time someone mentioned the serpents, Mitch grew more irritable.

Tommy wanted to crawl under one of the boulders and hide from what he'd done. They were stuck here because of him, because of his stories, and his dog's spaceship. Like the turtle in the woods, they were probably going to die because of him, too.

Unable to shake the chill from his dip in the ice, Tommy sat on a rock near the others and wrapped his arms around his body. "I'm sorry, guys. I got you all into this. It's my fault."

"No, it's not, kid," said Mitch, hefting a rock toward Shipwreck Lake. "It's my fault. We should've left when we had the chance."

Awkward silence filled the still air. "And, uh, sorry I knocked you out."

"Well, I guess I punched you first," said Tommy. "Sorry about that."

"Really?" Chuckey asked, sounding surprised.

"No, actually it felt pretty good," Tommy admitted.

Mitch nodded in understanding.

Muggie patted Mitch's sore arm. "I'm sorry I beat you up."

"Right back at ya," said Mitch, wincing. "You go, Peats. Apologize for something."

"What? I didn't do anything."

"I'm sorry I didn't leave a note for Mom and Dad when I left," said Danny.

Scott held up his backpack. "I'm sorry I didn't bring more food and water."

Mitch threw another rock. "And Steiber, I'm sorry I kissed your girlfriend."

Muggie's face turned as red as her hair. "Mitch, just shut up about that."

Tommy's stomach suddenly ached, and not from hunger. "What are you talking about? When did you two kiss?"

Mitch looked genuinely confused. "You didn't know?"

"It was nothing," insisted Muggie. "Just forget about it."

"Whoa, you guys kiss one minute and fight the next," said Chuckey. "It's like you're married."

Tommy surged to his feet. "I'm gonna take a walk." He stomped toward a forest of tall boulders, forcing even, steady breaths. Of all the things that wouldn't be in his story, Muggie kissing that big bully was at the top of the list. He looked up at the unfamiliar sky, and realized that things had gotten about as bad as they could get.

"Tommy, don't be mad at me," said Muggie when she found him.

"Hey, it's none of my business who you kiss. He's tall and muscular and a jerk most of the time. I can see why you like him."

"Come on, Tommy, I could never like Mitch Steelmaker, *ne-ver*—hear the syllables."

"Then why kiss him?"

Muggie gave a heavy sigh. "Yesterday, when we were waiting outside the ship, he said he'd stop being mean to you if I kissed him. So I did. Then he said the kiss wasn't any good, and he took back his promise."

Tommy felt warm inside again, but not from anger. "You kissed that swine just for me?"

"It was stupid; I know. Besides, I'm a sucker for blue eyed space geeks."

Tommy held out his hand. "You're amazing, you know that?"

"I can't argue with that," she said through a smile. She clasped his hand and squeezed it tight.

Tommy suddenly felt a strange force pulling him toward her. His heart pounded in his ears. If they got any closer they were going to...

A bright silver star shot across the sky. Then it slowed, turned, and headed toward them.

"Angel!" cried Tommy. "She came back!"

Muggie raised an eyebrow.

"Don't worry, she's just an Elf," said Tommy defensively.

Try Not to Die If You Can Help It

Angel stood close to the Silver Bullet, as still as the desert air. The orange poncho was gone. Instead, a forest green jumpsuit hugged her small form. She looked neither happy nor sad, neither frightened nor angry.

"Mitch, let me handle this," whispered Tommy. He and Muggie had arrived at the landing site at the same time as the others.

"One way or the other, Steiber, we're goin' home," Mitch declared, with his laser rifle lowered but ready. He motioned to Angel with his hand. "Step away from the Bullet, Sunshine."

Muggie wrapped her arms around Danny protectively. "We could use her help getting home, Mitch."

"We'll figure it out," said Mitch. "Right now, I just want my ship back."

"She's not gonna leave us," insisted Tommy.

"She's done it before," whispered Scott.

Home, said Angel. It wasn't a word, really; it was a sound, like music. Yet somehow Tommy knew what it meant.

Help.

"Is she singing?" asked Danny.

"It's beautiful," said Muggie.

Tommy stepped closer to the Elf of Light. "Yes, we need your help, Angel. Will you take us home?"

"How can you understand her?" asked Muggie.

Tommy cringed. "I don't know. It's *really* freaking me out."

"You got to the count of five to move away from the ship, Angel," announced Mitch, pointing the gun at her. "One."

Need you. Help me.

"What did she say?" asked Chuckey.

"Two."

Tommy clapped a hand to his forehead. "Of course! She needs *our* help freeing the Elves on Grenatia."

"Three."

"Mitch, don't do anything stupid," warned Muggie. "Don't forget she blasted a serpent with one of her starbursts."

"Four," said Mitch sternly. "All she has to do is touch the ship, and she's gone again. Then we're stuck on Snake Pit Moon."

Angel moved, startling everyone. She walked gracefully up to the group, straight up to Mitch, and touched his broken arm with her illuminated hand. He flinched and then smiled, flexing his arm effortlessly. "Hey, she just fixed my arm!"

Need warrior, said Angel, looking at Mitch.

Mitch took off his sling. "What did she say about me?"

Tommy had never been more tempted to lie. "She said she needs...*the warrior*," he said, putting the last words in finger quotes.

Mitch puffed up. "Warrior? Well, that's understandable. After all, we're talking about a rescue mission. Although, technically, I'm the Captain," he said to Angel. "She knows I'm the Captain, right?"

"Mitch, even the serpents know you're the Captain," said Muggie.

Scott looked doubtful. "Correct me if I'm wrong, Tommy, but didn't you say we'd get killed if we went to her planet?"

Mitch clasped Scott's shoulder armor. "Not on my watch, soldier."

"And now we got Angel," said Chuckey. "She's like a reusable hand grenade."

"But the Droids could have an entire army there waiting for us," insisted Scott.

"No," said Tommy, thinking. "Only a small unit guards the imprisoned Elves on Grenatia. The Droids' fleet and most of their forces are fighting the Goblins for control of a nearby star system. I think we can do this."

Hurry.

"We need to go," said Tommy.

"Move out," ordered Mitch.

"All right," agreed Scott, walking to the ship. "But if this part of the story makes it into the comic books, I want a cut of the profits."

"Hold on there, Tommy," said Mitch, pointing in the direction of the Elven campsite. "You and Muggie need to suit up with armor and weapons. Under the circumstances, I don't think the Elven Guard would mind."

"Did you just call me Tommy?"

"Yeah, well, don't get used to it. You're Private Steiber from now on."

"Private?" repeated Tommy incredulously. "Well, that's just great."

* * *

Tommy experienced another elevator ride when the Silver Bullet lifted off Snake Pit Moon. As they entered space, a rapid sunrise filled the ship with soft light. Like the Silver Bullet's glow,

Tommy found the sun's gentle radiance familiar and reassuring, though he didn't know why.

The Bullet's passengers were a little less queasy this time, perhaps because of Angel's expert piloting. She knew all the right symbols to touch and all the right notes to sing. Her song was sweet and full of hope. It made the mission seem less dangerous.

Tommy ruffled Danny's hair. The little boy sat pouting, with his arms folded. Muggie had made him promise that he would stay on the ship when they reached Grenatia.

"It's not fair," he whined. "You guys get to wear armor and fight Doom Droids."

"Angel needs you to stay and guard the ship," said Tommy.

The Elf of Light gave Danny a wink, which seemed to raise his spirits. The little boy joined her at the console, watching her work and singing along.

"What's the plan, Private?" Mitch asked Tommy.

"Well, when we find the Elves, they'll be encased in crystallox. It's like being trapped in a giant diamond."

"How long can they live like that?" asked Scott.

"A long time, as long as they have access to direct sunlight. Elves are creatures of light: they can't survive without it. So the Doom Droids will have them outdoors, probably on a steep hill or on a low-lying mountain."

Angel nodded in agreement.

"How did you know that?" asked Muggie.

Tommy shrugged. "It's just in my head, like the other stuff. Besides, a low mountain is easy to defend, yet not too difficult for the

Droids to climb. Angel will land on the top of the mountain. From there, she'll be able to free the Elves. The Doom Droids will try to stop her, so our job is to provide cover for Angel. We must keep the Droids from capturing her in crystallox. If they do, it's all over."

"But she can just use her power to bust out, right?" asked Chuckey.

"I doubt it. The crystallox casing is too strong. Speaking of which, we better hope the Droids think we're Elves, too. If they do, they'll only be able to trap us in crystallox. If not..." Tommy knew all too well how deadly Doom Droids could be. Though his Elven body armor imbued him with confidence, he knew it provided little defense against their blasters.

"Tommy, there's still one thing you haven't explained," said Scott. "How will Angel free the Elves from the crystallox?"

"She'll tap into their sun, amplify its light, and send the energy down the..." Tommy's voice faded. Dread filled his stomach as he suddenly wondered what the task of channeling that much energy would do to the Elf of Light. Angel's grave expression confirmed his fears.

"You don't have to do this," Tommy exclaimed, kneeling at her side. "We'll find another way to free the Elves."

No time. They are dying.

"Come with us to Earth. You'll be safe there."

No choice.

"You're an Elf of Light. Of course you have a choice."

My destiny.

"No. It isn't in the story," Tommy protested, his heart breaking. Staring into her golden eyes, he couldn't ignore the truth: Elves of Light were born in times of need. For the Elven people, their need had never been greater than now.

Angel brushed a tear from his cheek. *Be brave. Need you. For me.*

Tommy managed to nod, determined not to fail her.

Somber silence filled the cabin, as if the others knew the Elf of Light's fate. Muggie touched Tommy's shoulder, her eyes questioning. Tommy shook his head; it was the only answer he could give.

"Is that Grenatia?" asked Danny moments later, standing on a seat and pointing to a gray planet in the distance.

Tommy cleared his throat, and said, "It couldn't be. Grenatia's an Earth-like planet, with forests and oceans." They continued to close in on the murky sphere. Clearly, it was their destination. "What happened to Grenatia?" Tommy asked Angel.

Goblins, she said with dissonant tones.

"What is it, Tommy?" asked Muggie.

Tommy now understood why Angel had said the Elves were dying. "The Goblins must have done something to Grenatia to cloud its atmosphere. The Elves are cut off from sunlight. It may already be too late."

The pace of Angel's music accelerated as she guided the Silver Bullet down to Grenatia's surface, her melody as ominous as the clouds that enveloped the ship.

Glancing at the others, Tommy saw that they looked as anxious as he felt. Flying blindly through this sea of gloom was sapping their courage.

"Don't worry. She knows what she's doing," he said, feigning confidence. "This will all be over soon."

The ship suddenly veered sideways, throwing everyone onto the floor, just as an explosion of green light flashed outside.

"Not that soon, I hope," said Muggie.

The ship veered again, dodging another green blast.

"They're firing at us way up here?" asked Scott. "We'll never make it to the mountain."

The next blast struck the Silver Bullet, jarring the vessel.

Angel's melody dipped low. The ship dipped along with it, almost like it was falling. The change in direction seemed to work, because the enemy fire stopped.

At last, they broke through the clouds and found themselves descending to a land lush with autumn colors. Angel leveled out the ship's course, skimming the treetops, while speeding ahead. In the distance, a mountain rose from the horizon. As Tommy had predicted, it was little more than an overgrown foothill—short in height and wide at the base.

Scott pointed to the mountain. "That must be it."

"We're supposed to land on *top* of the mountain," complained Mitch, his face colorless.

"Angel had to change course to avoid their cannon fire," guessed Tommy. "We'll just have to fly up to the top." He knew that would be harder than it sounded.

"I can see the crystals from here," said Chuckey. "Whoa, there must be thousands."

Even with overcast skies, the crystals reflected soft light, flickering like monochrome fireflies. Inside each was an Elf whose life depended on the success of Captain Steelmaker's troops and the Elf of Light. Tommy bit his lower lip, worried for them all.

Without warning, another source of light erupted from the mountain. The barrage of red laser fire struck the Silver Bullet, and left it shuddering. The ship slowed, and its light flickered.

Finally, they reached the base of the mountain and started their ascent. The Doom Droids were now clearly visible among the randomly scattered crystals on the mountainside, their complex forms moving quickly as they blasted the ship. The Silver Bullet struggled up the slope, its reliable drone faltering.

Tommy pummeled the ship's wall in frustration. "We're losing power!"

"We'll never make it to the top like this," said Mitch. "Abort the mission."

"We can't," said Tommy. "Without sunlight, the Elves will die. If we leave, they're history."

"If we crash, *we're* history," Mitch retorted angrily.

The ship lurched forward; its power revived. Tommy saw that Angel was responsible for the renewal. She was infusing the ship with her energy as light poured from her body into the console. However, Tommy's relief was short-lived. Angel's golden light dimmed, and she slipped to the floor.

Without warning, the ship went silent and dropped to the ground, bouncing and rolling like a golf ball in the rough. It came to an abrupt stop, wedged between several crystals.

The passengers untangled themselves from each other, while groaning about their bruised bodies.

"I don't believe this," cried Mitch, cursing. "I think I broke my arm again."

"At least the laser fire stopped," said Scott.

"Wake up, Angel," said Tommy, patting her hand as she opened her eyes. With her light subdued, she leaned heavily on Tommy and Muggie to get to her feet.

"Now what?" asked Muggie.

Tommy scanned the outside. "We have to get Angel to the top of the mountain. It's not far." He hoped it was true.

"All right, we move out in arrowhead formation," ordered Mitch. "I'm on point. Peats, Salinas, take the flanks."

"In English, Mitch," insisted Tommy.

"You and Muggie just stay in the center with Angel."

"We can't leave Danny here," whispered Muggie.

"It's the safest place for him," said Scott. "Droids can't get in here. Only living things can enter the ship." When Tommy gave him a curious look he added, "What, you're the only one who can figure this stuff out?"

"Here they come!" cried Danny, pointing outside.

Tommy's blood turned cold. Looking through the window, he counted five Droids approaching. Their tarnished metal bodies jogged up the rocky incline with difficulty. "We're in luck. They're having a hard time getting up the slope."

"But we're surrounded," groaned Chuckey.

"We're gonna need one of your starbursts, Angel," said Mitch.

Muggie shook her head adamantly. "She can't. She's too weak."

Through the glass, Tommy saw the number of Droids double. "What are we gonna do, Captain?"

"Lieutenant, I need some rapid firepower." With a nod, Scott pulled a long strip of firecrackers from his backpack. Looking at Muggie, Mitch added, "That is, if it's okay with you."

Muggie smiled, nodding her approval. "Aye, Captain."

"Fire in the hole!" hollered Mitch when he lit the fuse. With a forceful touch of the glass, he was outside throwing the firecrackers and ducking for cover. As hoped, the Doom Droids retreated at the sound of the explosions.

Tommy, Angel, and the others left the ship and took up positions behind boulders and crystals. When the Doom Droids reappeared, they were met with an onslaught of laser fire from Mitch's army. The Droids couldn't endure the assault. Their bodies short-circuited and their metal parts flew as they crumpled to the ground.

"Move out," ordered Mitch, leading the way. The group hustled up the grassy slope in a triangular formation, picking off Droids along the way.

"They're not so bad," boasted Scott. "Tommy, aren't the Doom Droids in your comics tougher than–" *Voom!* A blast of clear energy enveloped the tall boy in crystallox.

"Scott!" cried Chuckey, running to his friend.

"Keep moving, Private," hollered Mitch.

"We'll come back for him," shouted Muggie. "He'll be okay. Won't he, Tommy?"

"I hope so," said Tommy, blasting three Doom Droids.

Angel quickened her pace. The number of Droids increased, making it harder to fight as they ran. Mitch was the only one able to keep up with the Elf of Light. His rifle was brutally accurate against the hapless Droids in his path. Chuckey, however, fell far behind and soon became ensconced in a block of crystal.

Tommy was now the last of the pack. His legs burned as he ran behind Muggie. Together they protected the group's sides and rear against an ever-growing number of Droids. But the mountaintop was still far off. They needed to move faster.

Ahead, Mitch stopped, hunkering down behind a large group of crystals. When Tommy and Muggie arrived at the enclave, they found Angel cowering near the ground; her tiny form trembling. Her light bled into the crystals she leaned against, and the glow illuminated the graying figures inside.

"She just stopped. I don't know why," explained Mitch between breaths. He and Muggie continued to fire at the approaching Droids. "Vamos, Sunshine! We still got a ways to go, and these robots aren't getting any friendlier."

"Just give her a minute," insisted Tommy.

"She's frightened, Mitch," said Muggie. "Can you blame her?"

"Look, we're all gonna die if she doesn't get up there and do her thing. What's she waiting for?"

"It's going to kill her!" shouted Tommy.

Muggie gasped. "How can that be?"

"She's going to die, and she knows it." Tommy knelt beside Angel. She was facing the end of her life. *How long had she lived?* he wondered. *Had she ever known happiness?* "It's so unfair. She's innocent."

Angel's swollen eyes grabbed Tommy's, searching for strength. *Help me. Make me.*

"I can't," said Tommy, shaking his head stubbornly.

Be brave. Need you. For me.

Squelching a sob, Tommy grabbed Angel's hand and pulled her from her sanctuary. The others followed them. After a few steps up the slope, she needed no further encouragement. The Elf of Light bounded ahead, heedless of danger. Her speed came not a moment too soon, for a crystallizing blast nearly struck them both. The energy grazed Tommy's armor and pulled his rifle from his hand. He dove behind a small crystal. *Voom! Voom!...Voom!*

Voom! The Droids had him pinned. Peering out, he saw that his friends were gone and his rifle lay on the ground covered in crystallox.

"Spectacular!" he roared, stomping his foot. "This is *not* happening."

Unwilling to give up, Tommy dashed from his hiding place. *Bad idea*, he thought, as he came face-to-face with three Doom Droids.

"Think fast, Steiber!" shouted Muggie, tossing her rifle to him. In the same fluid motion, she attacked the Droids, toppling two of them with sharp kicks. Tommy blasted the other one, and he and Muggie were off running.

Tommy handed Muggie's gun back to her, in awe all over again.

"What are you looking at me like that for?" she asked.

"I've never seen you fight like that."

She tossed her hair. "Whatever."

Yellow light flashed near the mountaintop, illuminating the sky and clouds above. "Go, Angel, go!" shouted Tommy, knowing it was Angel's starbursts. Then, from the peak, a column of light shot towards the heavens, and burned a hole in the overcast sky. Sunlight poured down through the opening.

"Yes!" shouted Tommy and Muggie, hugging each other in celebration.

Tommy looked up again just as Angel's light went out. He held his breath, waiting. "No, no, no!" He refused to believe that she'd failed. His legs started running for the peak. "Mitch, don't let them get her! MITCH!"

Voom!

"C'mon Muggie," he called, glancing back. Like a punch to his stomach, Tommy's eyes found the crystal that held her prisoner. His knees buckled, sending him to the ground. "No! Not Carrie Anne."

Further down the slope, still more Droids approached, aiming for him.

Tommy tore himself away, and raced up the slope with leaping strides, while dodging blasts of crystallox with zigzagged steps. There was only one way to save Muggie, and that was for Angel to succeed. She had already made it to the top. She just had to keep trying.

Panic crept under Tommy's skin when he passed a tall crystal housing Mitch. He forced the feeling away. Angel could take care of herself. She had more power than a hundred laser rifles.

"Angel!" Tommy cried when he reached the peak. Rocks and Droid carcasses littered the sun-drenched ground. Overhead, the hole in the clouds began to close. Where was Angel? Leaning against a small crystal, Tommy's mind raced through the possibilities. Was she hiding somewhere? Had they taken her prisoner?

"Angel, where are you?" Tommy called with a passing glance into the crystal. Deep within, the Elf of Light stood frozen, her glow extinguished. Tommy's body crumpled. Panic reached his lungs.

"Angeeeel!" he screamed, pounding his fists on the jagged column until they bled.

She remained like a statue, with her arms raised to the sky, embracing her destiny.

Doom Droids approached. The metal monsters formed a ring that slowly tightened around the summit like a noose around Tommy's neck.

"Need you. Help me," he sang to Angel in her spellbinding melody. He knew the Droids were aiming for him. It would all be over soon.

All at once, the Droids turned away, firing down the slope. With a whir, the Silver Bullet rose over the mountaintop. It dipped low, flying a circular pattern through the line of Doom Droids. Droids and Droid parts flew in every direction.

"Go, Dan Man!" cheered Tommy, captivated by the ship's familiar glow.

With a surge of emotion, Tommy suddenly realized why the light from the ship and the sun above were so familiar. The light from Cujo's body that had infused him only days before had held the same warm radiance. That light had made it possible for him to see Cujo's visions and understand Angel's melodic words. And that light was still there.

Excitement raced through Tommy's veins. The light and the power were there, deep within him. *He* could free the Space Elves and his friends, even Angel. With that joyous thought, his body shuddered, and the light within him came alive.

Without hesitation, Tommy threw his arms skyward. Light erupted from his body like from a volcano, blasting through the clouds above. In turn, a mighty shaft of sunlight hammered down onto him, burning into his spirit.

Tears of joy and sadness poured from his eyes. He thought of Mom and how much he loved her. He thought of Muggie and his friends and how much he would miss them. And he thought of Cujo and how nice it would be to see him again when this was over.

Like a dam bursting, the sun's light exploded from Tommy's body, sending beams of energy in all directions. He saw the clouds burn away. He felt the crystals and the Droids dissolve to dust. He heard thousands of first breaths.

Finally, he burned out, like an overloaded circuit. A smile curved his lips before he fell to the ground, and then he faded away.

Don't Look Into the Light

Tommy had heard stories of what death felt like, so he wasn't surprised when he saw a bright light ahead. This part wasn't in his story either, but he was okay with that. His friends were safe, and the Space Elves were free to roam the galaxy again. It had been worth it.

Growing impatient, Tommy wondered why he wasn't moving. After all, wasn't he supposed to float into the light? Then an angel appeared, her warm smile reassuring, and her arms wrapped around him.

Wake, Loremaster, she sang, caressing his forehead with her warm hand.

Blinking his eyes, Tommy looked around. The Elf of Light held him close in her lap. Muggie, Danny, Chuckey, and Scott gathered close to hug him. After a long embrace and a shower of tears, Tommy looked beyond his shipmates. Elves, real Space Elves, encircled them.

Finally, Mitch pulled Tommy to his feet. "Well done, soldier."

"Tommy, we thought you were dead," said Chuckey.

"How did you...?" started Muggie, wiping her eyes.

Tommy shrugged. "I couldn't let the story end badly. My readers would never forgive me." He wanted to tell them more, to share with them what he thought had happened. However, dizziness, exhaustion, and a jumble of emotions kept him silent.

The Elves, who'd gathered on the mountaintop and beyond, bowed to the Elf of Light, singing their thanks in chorus. Angel sang a response, bowing first to her people and then to Tommy. The Elves joined her, thanking Tommy and the Silver Bullet crew in jubilant song.

* * *

Descending Crystal Mountain, Tommy and the others watched the Silver Bullet swell to an enormous size on the plain below as Space Elves boarded the ship by the hundreds.

Mitch whistled in awe. "I should charge admission for this flight. I'd make a fortune."

"Can you imagine what the inside of the ship looks like now?" asked Scott.

"Yeah, think of all the bathrooms!" said Chuckey. "Hey, maybe there's a kitchen; no, a food court. I could really go for a cheeseburger."

Danny grabbed Tommy's hand. "I hope Angel lets me fly the ship home. I think I got the hang of it."

Tommy laughed, and said, "How did you manage that, anyway?"

"I *told* you; I'm a fast learner," insisted Danny.

"Tommy, what will the Space Elves do now?" asked Muggie.

"Well, they can't stay here. Their enemies are too close. When the Doom Droids learn of their escape, they'll probably come looking for them. But that may be the least of their worries. The Goblins are gaining strength again."

"So, what happens next, Tommy?" asked Danny, tugging on his arm.

Tommy didn't answer. He was too caught up wondering what it meant to be a Loremaster in these troubling times.

"I'll tell you what happens next," said Muggie, ruffling her little brother's hair. "We all go home and get in big trouble."

"Aw, I like Tommy's stories better," complained Danny.

Laughing, they headed for the ship and then for home.

* * *

After a short flight to a planet Angel called Eajewl, the Elves disembarked and boarded ships of their own. Eajewl had been a secret Elven base during the Droid wars. Fortunately, it had remained undiscovered by both Droids and Goblins.

Angel explained that the Elves would travel to a distant region of space and seek the help of their allies, the Centaurians. With any luck, the Doom Droids and Galactic Goblins would continue battling each other for many years. That would give the Elves time to establish a new home and begin recovering from their losses.

With the Elves gone, the Silver Bullet shrank down to its normal size, and Angel assured Tommy that the ship was ready to take him back to Earth.

To Tommy and his friends, this was welcome news. Though they enjoyed their time with the Space Elves, they were anxious to get back home. Eajewl was a swampy planet, rich with vegetation and infested with enormous mosquitoes. It proved to be as hospitable as Snake Pit Moon. But the truth was, even if Eajewl had been a space paradise, they still would have wanted to leave, as they knew their parents were distraught with worry. They had no doubt that search crews were combing Deep

Creek Woods by now as their parents feared the worst.

With firm tones, Angel instructed Tommy to keep the Silver Bullet safe. She expressed confidence that she would need his help in the future, and, when that time came, he would know what to do.

* * *

Within moments of departing Eajewl, the ship speeding through space, Tommy collapsed onto a padded bed that emerged from the cabin floor. He woke, after what felt like ages of sleep, to a darkened room and the sound of the ship's engines winding down. His crewmates were sound asleep all around him.

He saw darkness, not stars, through the panoramic window, and the muffled sound of rain filled the silence left by the now idle engines. Lightning flashed far away, giving Tommy a glimpse of familiar woods outside.

"Wake up you guys. We're back," he said, stepping over them. Perhaps it was the result of having flown billions of miles through space, but it felt to Tommy as though the ship were still moving.

The cabin's light level rose as the others woke, stood, and stretched.

Looking out the window, Chuckey asked, "Are you sure we're home?" Everyone responded by peering outside through cupped hands. Lightning flashed several times.

"Where else could we be with all this rain?" said Scott. "It looks like we're right back where we started; same hole and everything."

"Why do the trees look funny?" asked Danny.

When lightning flashed again, Tommy noticed it, too. Everything outside seemed to be leaning sideways. "We must've landed crooked."

Scott's brow furrowed over widening eyes.

"What's wrong, Lieutenant?" asked Mitch.

Scott looked at Mitch as if seeing right through him, then pressed his hands to the window and disappeared.

"Hey! I didn't give him permission to disembark." With a forceful touch on the window, Mitch disappeared, too.

Looking at her reflection in the window, Muggie combed her hair with her fingers. "Wait, guys! What are we gonna tell our parents?"

Tommy sighed, and whispered, "It doesn't matter. I'll be grounded forever."

"I don't care what they do to me, as long as they don't lock the fridge again," said Chuckey before vanishing.

Danny pulled his sister's arm toward the window. "C'mon, Carrie Anne."

Tommy blinked and the siblings were gone. He looked around the empty cabin for several long moments, reluctant to leave the

Silver Bullet. Mitch might be the Captain, but Tommy knew the ship was *his* responsibility. He felt certain he would need her again, and possibly soon. He wanted to stay longer, but his growling stomach goaded him into leaving.

Exiting the ship felt like stepping into a shower. Hard rain packed the darkness, making the shouts of his friends barely audible. What were they arguing about now?

"Tommy!" screamed Muggie as she pulled him away from the ship.

"We gotta get out of the woods!" yelled Scott.

Mitch was already forcing Chuck and Danny out of the ravine, hollering, "MOVE, MOVE, MOVE!"

"What's the rush?" asked Tommy, following his friends.

Scott hustled out of the ravine. "Mudslide! The trees are leaning down slope. It's a warning sign. This part of the woods could go any second."

Tommy felt his head shake in disbelief, even as he looked around at the legion of trees bowing deeply under flashes of lightning. It was as if the world had gone sideways.

Tommy glanced back at the Silver Bullet only to see its size diminish as it slowly sank into the mud. "The ship!" Its light flickered out just as he splashed into the mud next to it. "No!" He pounded the hull with his fists.

Muggie clawed at him, and hollered, "Let it go, Steiber!"

"I can't! I have to get inside...fly it away. Help me dig!" Tommy plunged his hands into the ground, scooping out mud again and again like a rabid steam shovel. But the ship sank deeper, and the earth shuddered far below.

"Tommy!"

Lightning struck with a deafening thunderclap, leaving Tommy stunned. He barely heard the pounding rain, the groaning trees, and Muggie's cries. Instead, Angel's words filled his ears with stark tones: *Need you again. Keep safe the vessel. You are Loremaster now.*

Tommy's cry of rage broke his reverie as the Bullet disappeared into the mud. A familiar force clamped around his waist, and lifted him up onto broad shoulders. Flailing his arms in protest, Tommy struck Mitch wherever he could. "Go back! We have to dig her out!"

Mitch dashed up and out of each ravine with relentless strides, his grip tightening as Tommy struggled to break free.

"Mitch, let me go! She has no energy field in the mud! She'll be destroyed!"

Looking back, Tommy glimpsed the lower woods as lightning flashed several times. His blood froze upon seeing the ground alive with movement; trees snapping, earth and timber tumbling into the gorge.

Mitch rolled to one side, dumping Tommy, as a tree crashed down beside them. The others screamed. Tommy scrambled on hands and knees, grabbing anything to pull himself forward, like clambering up a descending escalator. The ground rolled away beneath him. He braced himself for the ride into the gorge, wondering how they could survive the mudslide.

All at once, Tommy's hands clasped someone's shoulders as other hands found his arms. His friends were there in the darkness, pulling him and each other up the slope. Together, they ran until the forest floor lurched upward, throwing them down. The ground beneath them was solid but trembling. The earthquake echoed for what felt like ages as the ravines behind them crashed into the gorge.

Finally the rumbling stopped, leaving only the sounds of rain and heavy breathing.

More lightning revealed how close the group had come to death. As they climbed to their feet, they found themselves standing beside a massive oak. Its trunk was leaning over what was now a wider gorge.

Staring into the emptiness, Tommy tried to comprehend what had just happened. The Silver Bullet was gone, buried, along with Cujo's ashes, beneath tons of mud and debris. He would probably never see his ship again. Yet, somehow his heart burned with joy. He and his friends had made it home alive. The Elves were safe from harm, and even without a ship, Tommy knew his destiny as a Loremaster would find him again. In the meantime, he had fresh stories to tell and good friends with whom to share them.

He was suddenly aware of the many arms wrapped around him. Their warmth was a welcome comfort in the cold rain. "Let's go home, guys."

Epilogue

With muddy hugs and tears of relief, the group limped out of the woods and down the waterlogged streets of their neighborhood. As if on cue, the wind died down and the rain slowed to a drizzle.

Chuckey sighed as he patted Tommy's back. "Tough loss, man. It was an awesome ship."

"What do you mean, *was*?" grumbled Mitch. "The Bullet withstood laser fire from Doom Droid cannons. It can handle a little mudslide. We just have to dig it out, right Steiber?"

"Anything's possible," muttered Tommy, though he didn't believe it.

Scott chuckled. "Sure, we'll just get some industrial sized cranes and hire the Army Corps of Engineers. They'll have the Bullet out in no time."

"You really think so?" asked Danny, bouncing with energy.

Scott continued, "Of course, then the government will confiscate the ship and probably quarantine us for the rest of our lives."

Danny's energy evaporated. "That doesn't sound like fun."

"Thanks for getting me out of there, guys," said Tommy with appreciative looks at Muggie and Mitch.

Muggie smiled and held his hand, while Mitch clapped his back. "I gotta hand it to ya, kid. You're one brave soldier."

Tommy faked a punch to Mitch's arm. "Does this mean you're not gonna kick my butt the next time I'm in Deep Creek Woods?"

"I think we're all done being in Deep Creek Woods," said Muggie. "Now we're just in deep trouble." She pointed down the street, where several police and emergency vehicles were parked near the Muglyn home. Their lights flashed in the misty air.

Tommy's *I'm in big trouble* meter spiked. "How *are* we gonna explain being gone all this time?"

"Obviously, we were lost in Deep Creek Woods," said Scott. "I mean, we can't tell them the truth."

"I wish we could," said Tommy, knowing how much he hated lying to Mom. "But you're right; they'd never believe us."

Mitch raised a hand. "I'll take responsibility and tell them I led you guys the wrong way, and that we ended up lost south of the river."

Tommy clasped an arm around Mitch's shoulders. "How about we tell them we *all* got lost and *you* led us back home? That ought to look good on your Army application, eh Captain?"

Mitch shook his head. "I'm not joining the Army." Everyone stopped, stunned by his announcement. "I'm thinkin' Air Force; maybe even an astronaut."

"But you hate space travel," declared Danny.

Mitch shrugged. "It kinda grows on ya."

They managed to approach the Muglyn's house without notice. People were everywhere—officials in uniforms, neighbors huddled under umbrellas, children running about.

Passing a local news truck, Tommy stopped to listen to a reporter as she spoke to a camera.

"The children were last seen near the woods on Tuesday," she droned into her microphone. "Authorities are gravely concerned, as heavy rains have increased the chances of mudslides along the Lothlem Gorge from the county line all the way to the Cherokee River. Search and rescue efforts were suspended Wednesday night when more thunderstorms rolled into the area, bringing torrential rain. With the storms expected to move out of the region tonight, teams are planning to resume their search in the morning with the assistance of cadaver dogs."

"There they are!" hollered Mr. Beaker, startling Tommy.

Within moments, he and the others were surrounded by people. Questions flew faster than Tommy could hear them. Paramedics wrapped them in blankets, and police officers did their best to control the crowd. Tommy didn't say a word until Mom found him. Her bear hug embrace left him gasping.

"I'm so sorry," he pleaded again and again as she sobbed into his hair. His heart grew heavier the longer she cried. He could only imagine what she'd been through the last three days and nights. Glancing around, Tommy saw his friends reuniting with their families amid tears, hugs, and a few reprimands.

When Mom finally pulled away, she looked him over, paused on his sore eye, and touched it gently.

"I'm fine, Mom. Just a little hungry."

"Cujo?" she asked sympathetically.

With a forced smile, Tommy found himself looking back toward the woods, realizing something for the first time: Cujo—his dog, his friend, and in some ways, his mentor—had succeeded in his mission after all. The ugly mutt had protected Tommy. He prepared him for the dangerous trip to Grenatia with dreams of the Elves and their plight. Even more than that, Cujo's love and light had made it possible for Tommy and his friends to rescue Angel and free her people.

Turning back to Mom, and with his hand on his aching chest, Tommy said, "Cujo's here with me now. He'll always be a part of me."

Fresh tears welled up in Mom's eyes. "You kids went looking for him, didn't you?"

Tommy shrugged. "Well, sort of."

Mom swallowed hard and seemed to bury her anger. "I'm just glad you're all safe. Sheriff Rawlinson had half the county out combing the woods for you kids. Where *were* you?"

Tommy's mouth gaped open as he searched for words. How could he explain what had really happened? How could he tell her the truth without it sounding like a lie? If only he could show her the Silver Bullet, but it was gone.

After a long sigh, Mom ruffled his hair, and then hugged him again. "You know what, Blue Eyes? It doesn't matter. You're home safe, and that's all I care about."

"Mom, we found a spaceship!" he whispered, unable to hold back any longer.

"A spaceship?" she erupted. "Oh, Tommy, please don't start with stories about space people and–"

"Shhhh!" urged Tommy. He would have continued, with the dam inside him having burst, but Sheriff Rawlinson was approaching. She had wrapped up her conversation with the Muglyns, and she was headed toward him, followed closely by two officials in black trench coats. The hair on the back of Tommy's neck prickled at the sight of the grim-faced men.

Talking to the sheriff turned out to be easier than Tommy had expected. Much like Mom, she seemed to be most concerned with the fact that the kids were out of danger, though she reprimanded Tommy for hiking near the gorge, a place well known for mudslides.

As they spoke, the throng of neighbors thinned out; the paramedics packed up their gear; and the news vans drove away. The men in the trench coats stood back, listening and taking notes. Finally, when the sheriff seemed satisfied that she had all the information she needed, she turned to leave. The trench coats followed her. Almost as an afterthought, the taller of the two men looked back, and his eyes fixed on Tommy's feet.

"Excuse me, Ms. Steiber," he drawled as he flashed an FBI badge. "I've got just one more question for your son. Say, Tommy, where'd ya get those fancy boots?"

Tommy's heart skipped a beat. He was still wearing the armored boots from Snake Pit Moon. Though caked with mud, their Elven design and silver flair made them unlikely footwear for the average teenager.

Before he could answer, the other FBI agent pulled a wand from his coat pocket and waved it around Tommy; a wire connected the wand to a chirping metal box strapped to the agent's side. The instrument's random beeps grew louder as the wand neared the boots.

"What are you doing with that thing?" protested Mom, stepping between the wand-wielding agent and Tommy.

Ignoring her, the man wiped his balding brow with his sleeve, looked at his taller partner, and nodded.

"Forgive me, Ms. Steiber," said the first agent, the twang in his voice even stronger, "but I'm afraid a few more questions are required."

"What's this all about?" demanded Mom.

The agent continued, "Are you aware of eyewitness accounts of an unidentified aircraft in this vicinity the day the children disappeared?" Meanwhile, the balding man pressed a walkie-talkie to his mouth, rattling off number codes and top-secret lingo.

Mom rolled her eyes with a chuckle. "You're kidding, right? Look, don't put any more ideas in Tommy's head. All he talks about is stories about space battles and—"

"Ma'am, to the best of your knowledge, has your son or any of his friends ever reported seeing unusual, or possibly extraterrestrial, objects or creatures in this area?"

"Mister, if Tommy ever came across anything out of the ordinary, he'd tell..." Mom spun around to face Tommy, her eyes widening like blossoming flowers.

Tommy flashed her his best *I tried to tell you* look.

Mom glanced down at the boots, and then, as if achieving an overdue epiphany, mouthed, *the metal detector*. She turned back to the FBI agents. "I want to speak to Sheriff Rawlinson. You have no right to interrogate me or my son like this."

"Ms. Steiber, I do apologize. Your frustration is quite understandable, given all that you and Tommy have been through. However, your son may have been exposed to toxic and possibly radioactive contaminants during his *hike* through the woods. Might that be correct, Tommy?"

"We have a confirmed ETL in the Cherokee River Basin," announced the other agent into his radio. "I repeat. We have an ETL."

"Roger that, Foxtail," blared a response from the radio's speaker. "Hazmat teams approaching your location."

"Tommy," whispered Mom, her voice thick with fear. "Please tell us what happened."

Tommy looked away, facing the after-storm breeze, the kind that carries orphaned rain drops too tiny to matter. Overhead, the clouds were already breaking, and stars were peaking though their black openings. The tiny lights seemed to speak to him, twinkling assurances that everything would be all right. But a distant sound, growing stronger each moment, told Tommy otherwise. As the helicopters drew near, he looked down at his boots, painfully wishing he had left them on the ship.

The tall agent sighed. "Now, Tommy, I'm gonna ask you again. Exactly where did you find those boots?"

Tommy faked his best laugh. "What, these old things? Seriously, Mitch Steelmaker gave them to me. He must've got 'em at an Army surplus store or something."

The man honed his gaze on Tommy, his eyes as hard as steel. "Are you gonna stick to that story, son?"

Tommy smiled. "It's funny you should put it that way."

Acknowledgments

I wish to thank my family and friends, and others, for their support and encouragement as I've worked to bring this story to print, especially Dee Densmore-D'Amico, Jennifer Edwards, Chris Ernst, Mae Ernst, Nathan Ernst, Rob Ernst, Tara Gerner-Ziegmont, Seressia Glass, Kristen Ingmire, Maddy Ingmire, Lynda Love, Beth Major, Jeremiah Murphy, Karen Neitzel, Meg Schuessler, Gina Smith, Emily Trivitt, Katie Wright, Ryan Wright, and my parents, Richard and Patricia Ernst.

Moreover, please know how much I deeply appreciate you for reading my story. If you enjoyed it, leave a comment on my web site (www.drakehighlanderstories.com), and tell your friends, parents, teachers, librarians, and favorite bookstore manager about this book. Most importantly, keep reading, for the more you read the more you'll learn and understand about yourself and the world we all share.

About the Author

Drake Highlander's desire to write for children came alive while teaching middle school reading and social studies. In addition, many of his ideas are inspired by his own childhood experiences growing up in a large, close-knit family, and all the outrageous things that went on in that wonderful chaos.

Drake lives in Atlanta, Georgia with his daughter, Mae, and his beta fish, Boomer.

About the Illustrators

Cover art and design by Ryan Wright (www.ryryart.com)

Ryan Wright has always had a passion for art. His mother, an avid painter and art teacher, was a source of inspiration during his youth. Ryan's art has been applied to feature films, including Disney's *The Chronicles of Narnia*, *Dr. Doolittle 2*, and *The Aviator*.

Ryan lives in Atlanta, Georgia, with his Jack Russel Terrier.

Illustrations by Dee Densmore-D'Amico (deedamico.com)

Dee Densmore-D'Amico's work has appeared in publications such as *Cosmopolitan*, *Women's Wear Daily*, and *Modern Dog Magazine*. She has sketched in the design studios of well known fashion designers, including Diane von Furstenberg. In addition, she has received numerous awards from

Parenting Publications of America. Dee's major influences are Picasso, Antonio Lopez, Hirschfeld, Erte, and Dr. Suess.

    Dee lives with her family in central New York.